Mosquitoes

John R McKay

© Copyright 2016
John R. McKay

The right of John R. McKay to be identified as author of this work has been asserted by him in accordance with the Copyright, Designs and Patents Act 1988.

All Rights Reserved

No reproduction, copy or transmission of this publication may be made without written permission.
No paragraph of this publication may be reproduced, copied or transmitted save with the written permission of the publisher,
or in accordance with the provisions
of the Copyright Act 1956 (as amended).

Any person who commits any unauthorised act in relation to this publication may be liable to criminal prosecution and civil claims for damages.

A CIP catalogue record for this title is available from the British Library.

This is a work of fiction. Names, characters, businesses, places, events and incidents are either the products of the author's imagination or used in a fictitious manner. Any resemblance to actual persons, living or dead, or actual events is purely coincidental.

ISBN-13: 978-1523965861

ISBN-10: 152396586X

For Dawn

CHAPTER A1
The White Room

I start my day exactly the same way I have been starting my days for the past seven weeks. I wake up in floods of tears for no apparent reason that I can work out. I have never heard of this phenomenon before and I can find nothing on Google or Ask Jeeves that can help me to understand it. Even Mister Andrews has struggled to find a cause for it and if he doesn't know, then let's face it, nobody will. Maybe I am unique, maybe I am a freak of nature. Or, more than likely, maybe I'm simply just going mad.

Mister Andrews says that I must stay here just a little longer, to try to establish the cause of my recent odd behaviour but each time I ask him for a time frame, he fobs me off with 'soon' or 'we are just going to run a few more tests' or the worst one, the most patronising of all, 'until you are better, we wouldn't want to let you go too soon now, would we?' as though I am a small child, hankering for a lollipop which the kind man will give me if I do as I'm told, like in the dentist's or something.

How I have ended up in here is still a bit of a mystery to me. You can't call what I did a crime exactly. Okay, that's strictly not true. I suppose you could if you were being totally literal about it. But I didn't harm anyone, not physically anyway, I don't think, and if I offended anybody with my actions then so what. They are big boys and girls now. Be offended. People are too soft these days. Deal with it.

I lie in the bed with its starched white sheets reflecting the sunlight back through the large window to my left, as though this whitewashed room is trying to expel the invasion of summer that has entered like an unwelcome guest.

I take in my surroundings, just like I've done every morning for over fifty days now (I know, I've been counting), and I'm bored with what I see. It's a simple room, not much to it really. I have a small cupboard on either side of the bed on which are placed the few items I'm allowed to have. To my left there is a plastic cup, a plastic jug of water and a plastic bottle of orange squash. Two or three books that I have been given, that I have no intention or inclination of ever reading, rest unlooked at on the cupboard to my right. That's about it. That's all they'll allow me. Call it what you will… comical… pitiful… necessary?

A pasty faced woman wearing all white enters my white room and places a white tray containing eggs and white bread to the side of me. She avoids eye contact until the last minute, just as she is about to close the door behind her. I cannot make out if it's a look of revulsion, curiosity or pity. I hope to God it isn't pity, that would be awful.

I pick up the tray and start to eat. Thankfully the eggs are still warm and slither down my throat easily. The sliminess of the white, where it hasn't been cooked fully (my sister used to tell me this was bird snot when I was a kid), catches in my throat and I feel like vomiting it back up. I grab the beaker of water that I poured the previous night and slurp at it hungrily to wash it down.

I push the tray to the side and lie back against my pillow again and close my eyes. When Mister Andrews comes round later, which he is bound to do, then I will demand to know when I can leave. This is getting ridiculous.

An hour or so later, I can't tell exactly how long, I am awoken by the door opening and the same pasty faced woman who has been providing me with food and drink since I got here, (well most days anyway, they occasionally give her a day off), enters the room along with two other people. One is another woman, dressed just like her but infinitely prettier and a man I have never seen before, who carries a clipboard which he looks at thoughtfully through small spectacles that balance precariously at the end of his nose. I see that he is quite young, a lot younger than Mister Andrews and too young to have such a ridiculous haircut. He is bald on top and has allowed the sides and back to grow relatively long. I want to shout at him, 'Shave it off man, shave it off, you look like a prick' but I suppose my medication has stopped me from doing so.

My guard is instantly raised. Incidentally, both the women avoid looking at me and stare vacantly out of the window or at some inanimate object within the room, neither of them prepared to look directly at me.

I say nothing and join the women looking out of the window at the white clouds that pass lazily across my vision, as though they too are bored with the scene taking place within this room.

Eventually Mister Spectacles moves his eyes from the clipboard and looks over the top of his glasses at me. I can't make out what exactly it is he is thinking or indeed, what exactly he is doing here.

'How are we feeling this morning?' he asks in a strong southern accent. The kind that us northerners consider posh.

'Well I know how I'm feeling, but I can't answer for you,' I insolently reply. It has always annoyed me, this turn of phrase. Using "we" when you mean "you". It's ridiculous. As though using the plural for some reason makes him empathetic to what is happening to me. It's stupid and I hate it.

'Quite,' is all he can manage in response and looks down again at the clipboard.

'Where's Mister Andrews?' I ask after a few moments. 'I thought Mister Andrews was coming to see me today.'

Without looking up he replies, 'Mister Andrews is off for a few days. He won't be back until next week, so you will have to make do with me until then I'm afraid.' In no way does he say this apologetically.

'Well Mister Andrews said that I could be out of here very soon,' I reply.

'Have you been taking your medication?' he asks, ignoring me.

'Yes,' I reply. 'Of course I have. They tell me to take it, I take it. It's as simple as that.'

'It is,' he says. 'It's all very simple really. Why do you think that you will be allowed out of here soon? I'm sure Mister Andrews wouldn't have told you that.'

'Well he did,' I respond, getting agitated. I can feel the anger starting to rise inside me and I take a breath to control it. 'I need to get back home. I've a thousand things I need to do.'

The man, who still hasn't introduced himself to me, puts the hand holding the clipboard down to his side and looks over at me, a serious expression on his face.

'Are you aware of why you are here?' he asks.

'Yes I am,' I say. 'I know I have upset a few people but I'm sure they'll get over it. I've had a bad time recently and think I may have had a bit of a breakdown.'

'Mister Sumner,' he says calmly. 'Alex… It was a little more than a breakdown, I'm afraid. Can you not remember what it is you've done?'

And then it hits me like a sledgehammer. This is the same conversation I have had numerous times with Mister Andrews over the last few weeks. Each time the same words said in the same way and in the same tone as this bald moron is now using with me.

I say nothing and look again at the room I am in and realise why it is that the two women cannot look me in the eye. I see the bars on the windows that until now have gone unnoticed, my mind choosing to ignore them and I feel the tightness of the handcuff that chains my left hand to the bars of the bed. But worst of all… worst of all… I remember what it is that I have done which has led me to be here.

'Mr Sumner,' says this doctor, psychiatrist, or whatever the hell he is. 'Mister Sumner, you seriously assaulted your wife.'

CHAPTER B1
The Menagerie

2 Months Earlier

Another tedious day in the office.

Another tedious unnecessary meeting to waste my time when I could be doing something infinitely more constructive. The same usual tripe being spouted by the same usual tripey people who pretend to look attentive, important and serious as they peer over their glasses (if they wear them) while scraping pens across paper, making notes in a feeble attempt to make themselves appear more important than they actually are. And they expect my opinion, or at least some kind of contribution, but if I give it to them they will not like it, so I suppose it's best if I just keep my mouth shut and sit here pretending to be interested like the rest of them. Better to sit here like a mute idiot rather than upset these buffoons who pay me my pitiful wages.

I look around the room at this menagerie of humanity and hope that my contempt does not show too obviously upon my face. At the head of the table, like some self-important matriarch, sits the head of Human Resources, Felicity Henderson. Her appearance reminds me of Dustin Hoffman in Tootsie complete with glasses too big for her piggy little face. Her condescending and superior demeanour have accompanied her into the meeting and she smiles patronisingly at anyone who has the audacity to speak, or offer an opinion not in compliance with her own. She waves her hand dismissively, an insincere smile on her face, to anyone who has the nerve to actually say anything at all. She really is a nauseating little woman.

To her right sits Anthony Speakman, my immediate boss. I normally have a lot of time for Anthony but recently, since the announcement of the upcoming merger, he seems to have become more and more distant, as though the weight of the world is on his shoulders, but I have come to realise that he is looking out for himself and I have found it harder and harder to hold a conversation with him. He is the kind of manager who lazily uses the phrase "it is what it is" rather than deal with a problem. An idiotic phrase used by inept people who are in jobs above their intelligence level. The man is clearly worried about his own position within the organisation and who can blame him? Henderson has been gunning for him since the moment she arrived. Whether she sees him as a threat or an irrelevance I am not entirely too sure. An irrelevance probably.

Next to Anthony and to my immediate left sits a girl from Corporate Communications whose name I can't quite remember. Like all the girls who work in that department she is pretty, fresh out of university and has no clue about the world and how it works, or indeed, what exactly it is she is supposed to be doing. Why they have given these jobs to such people is beyond me but they seem to be springing up all over the place at the moment.

Across the table sit three more people. Another overpaid, nameless, waste of space from Human Resources who has been drafted into this meeting just to take the minutes, attempts to look important whilst she writes hurriedly onto her pink flowery notepad, trying desperately to keep up with proceedings. I make a mental note that if I do decide to say anything then I will say it as fast as I possibly can just to see how quickly she can write. I know this is extremely childish but you have to get your amusement from wherever you can in this godforsaken place. (It seems nowadays that you have to leave your sense of humour at reception as you come into work in the morning and then collect it again on your way out).

Sitting next to her is the guy from IT who I always forget the name of. Its either Gerard or Gerald, I'm not too sure. He is overweight with curly dark hair and a bulbous nose that seems to constantly glow bright red. Cracked veins on his cheeks give away that he has a severe alcohol problem to go with his body odour and halitosis issues, issues that he himself is quite oblivious to. I can see the minute taker turn her head away from him every time he speaks and who can blame her? It's enough to strip the paint from the bloody walls.

Sitting next to Gerard or Gerald or whatever the bloody hell this smelly bastard's name is, is another guy, John Michaelson, head of accounts, who looks at me with a knowing smirk every time Henderson opens her facetious, ugly, thin-lipped mouth. He is about the only one here, besides myself, who is actually worth the money they are being paid.

Sitting next to John is another complete loon. This is Annette Foster, Felicity's deputy who holds the title of "Office Manager" but, let's face it, everyone knows she is just a glorified clerk. She is one of those people who are eternally happy and smiley and optimistic. In short, a bloody irritation. She is absolutely useless at her job but at least her emails give us all something to laugh at. Her grammar is atrocious; she has no clue as to the difference in the words "there" and "their" or "where" and "were" (and "to", "too" and "two" come to that). She also constantly uses the word "of" instead of "have" which totally gets on my wick. To add to this, she always signs off with the acronym "P.M.A. peeps" (Positive Mental Attitude), as though her little pep-talk emails are actually taken seriously. Clueless. Bloody clueless!

And finally at the bottom of the table, facing Felicty Henderson, sits Eileen "Feed It Back" Ferguson, project officer for the upcoming merger. She is very small, thin as a rake and has no lips. Well that's not totally true, she does have some but they are very thin and she wears no lipstick so you can't bloody well see them. The lipless wonder.

However, I always try to be pleasant to her, my very job could depend on it, but in reality, like most of the others around this table, I have little time or faith in her. She never seems to have a straight answer for anything, always constantly checking and re-checking facts and never replying to emails, probably hoping that we'll eventually forget we've sent them. Awkward questions are not to be answered, seems to be her work ethic. The stock answer for any criticism, question or suggestion is 'I'll feed that back.' (I presume she means to the project team). Absolutely, totally and utterly bloody winds me up!

I suddenly become aware of all eyes looking at me. Henderson stares at me expectantly, waiting for the answer to a question I have not heard. I have not been listening. Why would I? This is totally boring and a complete waste of time.

'I'm sorry, Felicity,' I say casually. 'My mind was out of focus there for a second. Could you repeat the question?'

She smiles again but I know she is not happy. 'Yes, Alex, of course,' she says with more than a hint of condescension. 'I so like repeating myself. I was asking when you think that you will have the results of the staff survey available for us.'

Conscious of the promise to myself to speak as quickly as possible, I set off. 'Well Felicity, there are many who have either not yet completed it, have yet to send it back to me or have no intention of completing it at all. To be honest, as I'm sure you know, the morale of the workforce is at an all time low at the moment. Whether that's due to the upcoming merger and where that will leave them in the organisation, whether it's down to the fact that they are unsure if they even have a future here, because, let's face it, when these things happen there always follows restructuring of some sort and that always means job cuts. Or whether, and this I believe to be the case more than the other two points I have just made... '

'Alex, Alex,' she says holding up her hand. 'Please slow down. Poor Julie is struggling to keep up.'

I look across at "poor Julie" who is scribbling as fast as she can with a pen that obviously has given up on her, because she is shaking it up and down in attempt to get it to work again. The only words I can think of are "mission accomplished" but for some reason the sensible part of my brain takes over and out loud I say: 'Sorry Felicity... Julie... I'll try to slow down a bit.' I catch John's eyes and he looks down, his hand covering the smirk he is trying to hide from 'she who must be obeyed' at the end of the table.

'Like I was saying,' I continue, keeping my face perfectly straight, 'I believe the indifference of the workforce in completing the survey is down to there being no confidence in the current management team.' I look over to Eileen Ferguson. She starts to mouth 'I'll feed that back,' but I turn away from her before she has chance to finish it.

For the first time Felicity's expression changes. She looks personally affronted. Which, truth be told, is exactly what I was trying to achieve.

'And what makes you say that?' she asks.

'Well it's quite obvious to those of us who have been here for many years,' I say, (knowing that Felicity has been employed here for barely six months). 'Up until quite recently the morale of the place was very high. People used to love working here. But for some reason, and I don't think this is all down to the merger, that morale has fallen sharply. I overhear things... Come on now,' I look around the room for back-up which does not arrive, 'you've all heard what they are saying, surely. I'm not making this up.'

'Does anyone else see this?' interrupts Felicity-bloody-Tootsie.

Blank faces look back at her. She looks at me again.

'Maybe you have a bit of an overactive imagination, Mister Sumner,' she says in that patronising manner we have reluctantly got used to and are forced to tolerate. 'I do hear that you are something of an amateur novelist. Maybe you are dreaming this up.'

My anger rises. 'No Felicity… Mrs Henderson.' (Well if she is going to address me by surname then maybe I should do the same to her). 'I am a novelist in my spare time, it's a hobby and has nothing to do with this. But if you want me to answer your question honestly then allow me to do so. If you don't want to hear an honest answer then please don't bother asking me the question in the first place. I'm not the type to tell you what you want to hear if it isn't the truth.'

There is shock on the faces of all around the table. No-one has ever spoken to her like this. No-one has ever had the balls before. Well… she gets on my bloody nerves and I am glad I have said it.

There is an awkward silence. No-one seems interested in speaking next. Felicity looks at me with that strange smile on her lips but I look down at my notes and ignore it.

'Okay,' she says eventually. 'Does anyone want to add anything to that?'

Again silence from the rest of them. One or two shake their heads.

'In that case then I think we shall close the meeting. It's getting late in the day now anyway and I'm sure that you all want to get off home soon.'

The sense of relief is palpable and John and Gerald/Gerard push back their chairs and stand up. I go to do the same but Felicity holds out her hand to me, like a policeman directing traffic. 'Could I have a quiet word please, Alex?'

I long to say 'No you bloody well can't,' but I know it won't go down well. Instead I say meekly, 'Of course, Felicity.'

We wait a few moments as the others leave the room and wait again for the door to close behind them, which it does very slowly. Eventually we are alone and I can sense that she is not happy with me. But then I am pretty much past caring if I am honest with myself.

'Alex,' she says slowly. 'Alex. I need to speak to you about one or two things that may be happening around the office soon.'

A feeling of inevitability creeps into my thoughts. I have a sense of where this conversation is going to lead and I don't like it one bit.

'Go on,' I say looking at her.

'Yes, well. How can I put this?'

Come on, I think, spit it out woman!

'You touched on it just now,' she continues. 'Like you say, the merger will bring about certain restructuring issues. It's what those at the top are wanting. They have to make efficiency savings and such like, so I'm afraid that there will be a certain amount of redundancies. All voluntary of course.'

'Yes,' I say, dragging out the word. Come on just say it!

'The thing is, Alex. We are looking to change a few things around here and I'm afraid that there is a possibility that your post... your role, will be one of those that will be looked at.'

'Are you sacking me, Felicity?' I blurt out.

She looks genuinely taken aback. But then again she is a very good actress and Dustin Hoffman is one of my favourites! 'Goodness no,' she says. 'Of course not. What I am trying to say is that, moving forward, it may be a good idea for you to start looking at your options. Maybe now is a good time for you to start looking at the direction your career is taking and maybe... how shall I put this... find another path.'

'Can't you speak properly,' I say. 'This kind of management speak is ridiculous. Just say it how it is will you? Am I to assume that when the changes happen then I will be out on my ear?'

'Well I wouldn't have put it quite so colloquially,' she responds.

'Colloquially?' I reply. 'Colloquially? Do you even know what the word means?'

'Now, Alex, there is no need to be rude.'

'I'm not the one being rude,' I say in response. I can feel my temper rising and am doing all I can to keep it in check. 'I'm not the one telling me that my career is over, now am I? You are looking at letting me go and probably keeping on all those other useless knobs out there who don't know their arses from their elbows. And I know the reasons why. It's not because of my position being made redundant at all. It's because I'm the only one here who is prepared to tell you and the other buffoons in charge of this place what everyone else is thinking. But rather than sort out the problems you have, you simply get rid of those highlighting the issues. Useless bunch of fucktards the bloody lot of you.'

With that I push back my chair and storm out of the room. I would slam the door behind me but it has one of those strange contraptions at the top that ensure doors are always closed, I think its a fire containment thing, but it also serves to prevent the slamming of doors in situations such as this. Consequently the door merely makes a grating, grinding noise for a second or two before slowing down to a more relaxed closing, totally taking away my intended slam.

Am I glad I said it? Am I glad that I vented my spleen to old Tootsie in there? I'm not so sure but the one thing that I am absolutely sure of is that I need a drink. And I need one right now.

CHAPTER A2
Group Therapy

Doctor Spectacles looks at me from across the room and indicates for me to respond, but as per normal for me these days, my concentration has slipped and I have no idea of what it is he would like me to comment on.

There are around ten of us in the room, all sitting in a semi-circle facing him. Each one of us with our own particular issues. There is a huge male nurse standing at the door, his back to it with his arms folded, his short sleeve shirt tight around his oversized heavily tattooed biceps. I think he is called Ryan, or maybe Brian, or something like that, but then I suppose the bloke's name isn't really that important right now. What is important is getting "better" so I can get the hell out of this place. And if that means that I have to attend these idiot sessions with Spectacles and the other retards then I suppose it's just something I will have to put up with.

'I'm sorry,' I say blankly. 'I haven't been listening. Can you repeat the question?'

'You haven't been listening?' he asks, affronted.

'That's what I said, Doc. I see there's nothing wrong with your hearing.'

One or two laugh. Vivien guffaws. (Strange name for a man, I think, but then I'm not going to tell him, he has tattoos on his face and neck and anyone half-witted enough to do that is more than likely to be totally unpredictable).

'There's no need to be rude, Alex,' he replies and I have to admit that he has a point.

'I'm sorry, Doc,' I apologise. 'Sometimes I can't help myself.'

He looks at me over the top of his glasses and I wonder why he is wearing them at all if he isn't going to use them. 'And why do you think that is Alex?'

That, I think, is the million dollar question. I have absolutely no idea why I do this. I never used to be like this. As a child I would never have said boo to a goose, yet now, over the last few months, I have become very obnoxious, impertinent and sometimes just downright nasty. I have no idea why? It's come to the point that I even get on my own nerves.

'To be honest, I really don't know. Maybe circumstances have made me this way.'

'Yes, maybe,' he replies thoughtfully, eager to pursue this line of thought. 'But do you think that being a victim of circumstance makes it okay for you to be rude to people.'

'I suppose I have given up on tolerating fools. I've come across that many of them over the course of my life.' I look around the group. 'Present company excepted of course…'

'See,' says Spectacles, 'you're doing it again, Alex.'

'Am I?' I look around the group once more and notice that if I was being rude then none of them have noticed or are any the wiser. 'I don't think anyone has taken offence.'

'It doesn't stop it from being rude though. They could have quite easily taken offence. You weren't to know.'

I lean back in my chair. This conversation is starting to get on my tits. 'So what?' I say, maybe a little too loudly as I notice Brian or Ryan (or is it Dave? It could be Dave, thinking about it) suddenly look over and become more alert to what is happening in the room. I take a breath and try to calm down. 'So what if people get offended by some things I say. Everyone is too sensitive these days. If they are offended then I suggest that they stop being so bloody soft and deal with it. If you don't like what I have to say then just ignore me, or tell me to shut the fuck up. Don't just sit there crying to yourselves and then go home and tell your mums and dads. I think people have stopped knowing what it's like to be an adult these days.'

Spectacles is writing away furiously on a piece of paper on his clipboard. Eventually he looks up and then around at the group. 'Does anyone wish to respond to what Alex has just said?'

Eddie raises his hand.

Eddie Scraggs. I don't know what he is in this place for and to be honest I don't think he does either. His name conjures up visions of dirty fingernails and scabs and such like, and that is exactly what he looks like. He has a matted beard that he refuses to wash or shave off, his hair is long and thinning and he scratches incessantly at an eczema covered right leg that he digs into with his scabby nails, his trouser leg rolled up to his knee and bits of his skin flaking off onto the floor as he does so. He is revolting and if I owned a weaker stomach I'm sure that I would vomit every time I am in his nauseating presence.

Sitting next to him is Charlie Jones, the little Welsh dwarf (well he is actually around five feet four inches but that's dwarf enough for me). If Eddie is the monkey, Charlie is definitely the organ grinder and he looks at Eddie expectantly.

'Yes, Eddie?' says Spectacles, keen to involve as many of these freaks as possible.

'I'm a bit scared of him,' he responds and I nearly laugh out loud.

'What do you mean?' asks the Doctor, ignoring my muffled mirth, his interest at a heightened state of alert. He leans forward in his chair.

'Well,' Eddie continues. I can tell he is aware of me staring at him but he avoids looking my way. Am I really scary? That's one thing that I was never aware I could be. 'He says that we should just deal with things and has no patience for other people. If I am offended by something he says, he just laughs at me and I find it a little scary.'

Spectacles turns to me. 'Have you anything to say about that?'

'I refer the honourable gentleman to the answer I gave some moments ago,' I respond in my best David Cameron voice. No-one laughs. No-one laughs because none of these thick bastards understands the joke.

'You're a tit,' says Charlie under his breath.

'And you're a dwarf,' I say louder.

He rises from his chair and starts to approach me. I lean back in mine and laugh as Ryan, Brian or Dave or whatever the bloody hell the big nurse's name is, comes forward towards us. Seeing him approach, Charlie sits back down.

'Calm down gentlemen,' says Spectacles. 'Let's keep this civil. Alex is there something you want to say to Charlie for that little outburst.'

'There's plenty I want to say,' I reply. 'For example, I want to say that if he ever calls me a tit again, or makes out that he wants to come over and punch me in the face then I will knock the living shit out of him. I also want to say that he is an ugly little bastard who manipulates poor scabby Eddie and should be ashamed of himself. But I suppose you will be pleased to know that I won't say any of that and like a good little conformist, I will merely say "I apologise profusely, my little chum, for any offence my little comment has caused you."'

I look over to Spectacles.

'There,' I say, 'will that do for you?'

CHAPTER B2
Literally Speaking

I walk into the George and Dragon desperately in need of that drink. The afternoon's meeting has been the usual complete waste of time. No decisions made as per usual, just a load of arseholes (with the odd exception) loving the sound of their own voices and spouting the usual shitty management speak that seems to have arisen from somewhere over the last few years. Expressions such as "thinking outside the box", "all of our stakeholders", "appetite for risk" and "thought showers" actually being spoken out loud, as though using these ridiculous buzzwords mean that they actually know what they are talking about when the truth of the matter is that they are using them to cover for the fact that are completely clueless and just want to impress the company bigwigs (who actually fall for this bullshit and even use it themselves).

I approach the bar and wonder if I have ballsed everything up. I'm not quite sure, and, truth be told, at this moment I'm not that bothered or worried. Felicity Henderson is a grade one idiot anyway and if I am to be made redundant then I know that I won't be out of work for too long. If she and the firm don't appreciate my skills then that's their problem, there will be plenty out there who will. That's their issue not mine.

As I get to the bar I see a few from the office in a corner drinking lager and laughing together as another throws his money away into a games machine, getting increasingly frustrated as his cash disappears amongst the flashing lights, buzzes and irritating little tunes that these machines spew out. I can see that Gerald/Gerard and my only real friend at the company, John Michaelson, are amongst them. I order a pint of lager and then walk over to where they are all standing.

'Bloody hell,' says Gerard or Gerald as I get near to them. 'Here he is, the man of the moment.'

The bloke is way too jolly for my current mood but I smile at him politely nevertheless. 'Well,' I say, 'it needed saying. Bloody stupid woman.'

'Oh, she's not that bad,' he responds taking a huge gulp from his pint glass. 'You need to relax and let it wash over you. She puts a front on sometimes just to make sure that everyone knows who the boss is. There's no real harm in her.'

'She's a nasty, spiteful, vindictive, waste of space,' I reply before turning away from him to speak to John.

'Did you know she used to be a cleaner until quite recently?' he tells me. 'Apparently she used to work down at the local police station mopping floors and dusting offices and all that sort of stuff.'

'Doesn't surprise me at all,' I reply. 'Not one bit. It's about all she's fit for. So how come she ended up in charge of us lot then?'

'No idea,' replies John, shrugging his shoulders. 'Not a clue. I suppose she must have taken some exams or courses or something and then got lucky.'

Gerard or Gerald steps between us, bored now with watching his mate pump pound coin after pound coin into the bandit for no return whatsoever. 'Yeah,' he says, 'I heard that too. What did she want with you after the meeting? I could tell she was fuming with you. Her eyes were like, literally popping out of her head!'

'Literally?' I reply. He is oblivious to my mocking tone.

'Yeah, mate, she was fuming.'

John looks at me. 'What did she want? Is it anything that any of us need to be worried about?'

I am aware of Gerard/Gerald/fat-red-nosed-irritating-tosser looking at me with an inane grin on his face, as though he is my new best mate or something.

Trying my hardest to pretend that he's not there I answer John.

'It looks like there are going to be a few redundancies in our department, maybe throughout the whole company. I don't know why she couldn't have told us all in the meeting but I suppose she wanted to have her moment of fun with me. I'm afraid I didn't handle it too well and I'm sure I'll be hauled in front of the bosses tomorrow.'

'Jesus, Alex,' says John concerned. 'What did you say to her?'

'Oh I don't know. Nothing that wasn't true. I think I might have called her a fucktard or something.'

Gerard/ld lets out a low whistle and John sprays a mouthful of lager onto the carpet in front of us. The barman looks over for a second but John holds up his hand in apology and so the man goes back to serving two girls who have just walked in.

'For Christ's sake, Alex,' he says, wiping his mouth with the back of his free hand. 'Are you trying to get yourself sacked? You walk a fine line as it is.'

'I'm past caring to be honest with you,' I say.

Gerard/ld is now smiling at me, his nose growing redder with each mouthful of beer he pours into his bloated face.

'Let's face it. She hates me and I hate her,' I continue. 'It's as simple as that. We both know where we stand. And if you want to know what she said to me... well she pretty much told me that when they announce the redundancies I am more than likely going to be on top of the list. I suppose it's one way of getting rid of me.'

'My God,' he says. 'What are you going to do?'

'I don't know. I suppose I'll just have to look for another job. Or maybe my novel will take off and I can do that for a living. Something will turn up.'

'How's that going?' he asks. I can see that he wants to change the subject. He looks awkwardly at Geraldy Gerard and I instantly know that something has been said before I arrived in the pub. But I decide to humour them anyway.

'Oh, it's done,' I reply. 'It's finished and edited. I have submitted it to a few agents and am waiting to hear back.'

'Well done mate,' he says patting me on the shoulder. 'And when do we get a chance to read it?'

'Not until it's published,' I reply. 'I know I shouldn't brag but it is quite good. Better than a lot of the other shit you can pick up in Tesco or Asda. I just hope it takes off.'

'Well I hope that it happens for you, mate, I really do. I'm really impressed that you've done it.'

'Yeah,' I reply, accepting his compliment. 'But I think I've pissed Jenny off with it. She says I've been obsessed. She goes out most nights with her mates but I haven't really bothered because it's meant that I can carry on and get it done. She'll thank me for it one day when I'm rich and famous.'

'Yeah, mate, she will. She will.'

'Anyone want a pint?' asks Gerardy Gerald.

We both tell him that we are fine and he leaves us to go to the bar. John and I step aside, away from the others who continue to laugh and joke like a bunch of kids near the games machine, just as it finally gives in and the "kerdunk, kerdunk, kerdunk" noise starts as it throws out all the coins that the guy has just put in. Pretty much a total waste of time. He's probably put in a tenner to win a tenner and the thick bastard actually thinks that he's up.

'What's that guys name?' I ask John, motioning to the fat red-nosed irritation that has gone to the bar.

'Jerry,' he replies. 'Why?'

'I wasn't sure if it was Gerard or Gerald.'

'Oh, right. Could be either I suppose. We all just call him Jerry.'

That's one thing sorted if nothing else.

Jerry returns and unfortunately decides to come and stand with us again, and not with the others who are still congregated around the fruit machine, all congratulating the player on his life- changing win.

'Did you see that bird at the bar?' he says, a look of glee in his eyes. 'Did you see her?'

'No,' we both reply in unison. John turns his head to look over but I am determined not to give the bloke the satisfaction.

'She was gorgeous,' he says. 'I was, like, literally standing there with my tongue hanging out.'

'Okay,' I say. 'Like literally?' He is not aware that I'm taking the piss, or if he is, he's ignoring me.

'Yeah,' he responds enthusiastically. 'She was literally Angelina Jolie!'

'Jesus Christ,' I say in mock shock. 'Did you ask her for her autograph?'

'Don't be stupid,' he says, looking at me as if I was exactly that. 'Why would I do that?'

'You said that it was Angelina Jolie. If I was stood in a pub next to a Hollywood superstar as she orders half a Guinness and a packet of pork scratchings, then I'd definitely ask her for her autograph.'

'Are you being funny?' he says, affronted at my piss taking.

'Clearly not,' I reply. Let's face it, no-one is laughing.

No sense of humour some people.

'I didn't mean it was, like, Angelina Jolie. I meant that it was someone who reminded me of her.'

'Then why say literally? You're confusing me now,' I respond. 'And why say you didn't mean it was someone "like" Angelina Jolie and then say it was someone who looked like her. You're not making sense.' I know I am playing with him and it won't be long before he gets really annoyed, but I'm having fun and after the day I've had today, I really could do with some.

'It's a turn of phrase,' he responds. 'Stop being a tool.'

'Now now, boys,' says John, raising his hand. 'Let's play nicely now.'

Jerry scowls at me and turns away to rejoin his friends.

'Why have you got to be like that Alex?' asks John, when he is out of earshot.

'Oh I don't know,' I say. 'I've had a bad day and I suppose I'm taking it out on the first knobhead I come across. Unfortunately for Jerry, Gerald, Gerard, or whatever the bloody hell his name is, he just happens to be here.'

'You should maybe take a holiday or something, mate. You seem really stressed out.'

I know this is a good idea and one that should be looked at, but it's hard enough these days to get Jenny to spend any time with me at all, let alone a full week or two on our own together, twenty four seven.

'A word of advice,' he says as I quietly sip my pint. 'You've got to be careful what you say. If you carry on like this you're going to make yourself unemployable in this sector. They'll not give you a good reference if you piss them off too much.'

'I don't care,' I reply defiantly. 'The people in charge of that place are all wankers.'

'I know they are,' he agrees, 'but you have to play the game if you want to get on. Otherwise they'll crucify you.'

I look at him and for some reason his words seem stupid to me. As though what he is saying makes no sense at all.

'I don't care,' I say, 'I have one life John... one. And if at the end of it I cant look at myself, then what's the fucking point in living it in the first place. Conform if you want. Kiss their arses if that's what suits you, but I can't do it. If I can't be true to myself then everything else that happens in my life is just false and bullshit. Life can't be just about being born, paying your bills then dropping dead. What's the point of it if it is?'

'How long are you out for,' asks John, suddenly changing the subject. Maybe I've touched a nerve with him. 'I'm going home after this one.'

'Jenny's out at aerobics or something tonight, so I might have a couple more. I'm driving though. so I might get a taxi and pick up my car tomorrow,' I reply thoughtfully. I've got the taste now, twenty quid in my pocket and time to kill. I might as well do it here.

Five minutes later John says his goodbyes and leaves and I try to re-integrate myself with the others. There are four of them in total, including Jerry the red-nosed wally. I join them mid conversation and it's clear that Jerry has had some good news.

'Hey, Alex, have you heard Jerry's news?' asks one of them, Liam, a red haired office clerk who wears a suit at least two sizes too big for him. In the office we call him "Liam Morris, Mr Grievance" for all the moaning he does to management about the most trivial of issues; his chair isn't right or the temperature at his workstation is too hot or too cold, that type of thing. His latest is trying to get his badge changed from saying "Admin Assistant" to "Admin Co-ordinator". Give me strength! Before Jerry can prevent him from continuing Liam blurts out, 'He's getting promoted. They've told him in the grand shake-up he's getting head of a department.'

Jerry looks physically uncomfortable as the others pat him on the back.

'That's nice,' I say, trying to maintain my dignity. 'Which department is that?'

'Oh, I don't know yet,' he says defensively. 'They're not sure. It depends on what happens with the restructuring.'

I am finding it difficult to maintain my composure. On the very day they tell me that they are probably going to let me go, they are telling this fat, useless, waste of space that he's getting promoted. It's surprising how far arse kissing and backstabbing can get you these days.

I hold out my hand to him. He takes it and shakes it limply. His hand is cold and clammy and I wipe it on my trousers when he turns his head away. One or two notice but I don't care.

'I bet you're made up,' I say.

'Yeah,' he says. 'When Felicity told me I was, like, literally over the moon.'

'So you were actually in outer space then, in a space ship or something?'

'No, of course not, you idiot.' He is getting annoyed with me again. Good. My plan is working. I'm determined to give him a hard time.

'Then why say literally?'

'Because it was, like, literally, mind-blowing,' he replies.

I turn my head away and mutter under my breath, 'For fuck's sake.'

'What was that? You taking the piss?' he says, finally understanding that I'm doing just that, and his whole face, not just his nose, is now as red as a huge beef tomato. He is very close to the edge and I am finding it all extremely funny.

'No, mate. It just irritates me when people say literally without knowing what it means.'

'Are you calling me stupid?'

'No. Did I say that? Did I say "Hey stupid, stop saying literally out of context?"' I reply. Everyone else is quiet now. No more playing on the fruit machine, which has fallen silent, glad of the rest from these morons, no doubt. They are all staring at us both in an awkward silence. I am also aware that it's not just our group that are looking at us, but others near to us have stopped talking to see how this develops.

'You're the stupid one, pal. Not me,' is his best response.

Oh hell, I think. Whatever. Go for it Alex.

'Why would you think I'm stupid?' I ask. 'Because I know what a word means and you don't? That makes you stupid if anyone is, not me. You don't understand what I say so you call me stupid when in fact, because you don't understand me, in my book, that makes you the stupid one.'

'You are starting to get on my nerves now,' he says threateningly.

'What, literally? Am I literally starting to get on your nerves? You see you didn't say it then, so do I believe you mean it or not? You're starting to confuse me.'

And then he punches me.

Hard.
In the face.
Like, literally.

CHAPTER A3
Mister Andrews

Mister Andrews is back from his holiday. He's obviously been away abroad somewhere because he has come back two shades darker than he was before he left. His shaven head is glowing a deep brown but his large, hooked nose looks slightly burned and out of synch with the rest of his face which makes it look slightly odd. He smiles at me through perfect white teeth. Teeth that are obviously not those that he has grown himself. They clearly pay these clowns too much.

'So, Alex,' he says. 'Before I went away we discussed why it was you think that this guy,' he looks down at his notes, 'Jerry... yes that's it... Jerry... why it was you think that he assaulted you.'

'Did we? I can't remember.'

'Yes, we did. But just before we come to that. Can you tell me why Doctor Green felt the need to place you in handcuffs a few days ago?'

'Shouldn't you speak to him about that?' I ask. Well, it's a perfectly good question!

'I have, but I would like to hear your take on it.'

I sigh. Here we go again. More bullshit mind games. 'Okay,' I say, 'If we must... To be honest I'm not a hundred percent sure. Apparently... I hear that some of the nurses have felt threatened by my behaviour. I have no idea why. I'm not a violent man in any sense of the word.'

'You attacked your wife, Alex,' he says, looking up. 'And others. They know this. It's part of the reason why you're in here.'

'So you say,' I respond. I really have no idea why he would think like this. Attacked my wife? Jenny? And others too? I have no memory of it.

'There were many witnesses, Alex,' he says. 'But we will come back to that later. You threw a tray at one of the nurses the other day. She had to run out of the room. She thought you were going to hit her.'

'A total misunderstanding,' I explain. 'She over-reacted. I get a little claustrophobic sometimes.'

'She didn't throw the tray, you did. Don't you think that you were the one who over-reacted?'

I can't argue with his reasoning. Instead I shrug. 'Well. I'm sick to death of those bloody runny eggs they keep bringing me. The least they can do is cook them properly instead of trying to give me salmonella poisoning or something.'

'Do you think that's what we're doing? Trying to poison you?'

'You're putting words in my mouth now. You're making out that everything I say has a literal meaning when the opposite is true,' I respond. 'Of course I don't think you're trying to kill me. At least I hope that you're not.'

He doesn't laugh at my small attempt to lighten the atmosphere which has gone decidedly frosty over the past few minutes. These sessions, like a lot of things these days, are starting to irritate me.

'Okay,' he eventually says. 'Let's get back to Jerry.'

'Oh, yes,' I say sarcastically, 'Please let's. I just love that man!'

He frowns but ignores my sarcasm.

'Why do you think he assaulted you?'

'I have a couple of theories,' I reply. 'It all depends on your point of view. You could argue that I was being rude and obnoxious and he was too stupid to be able to argue with me intelligently. You could argue that I deserved it, and that would pretty much be the truth, but you could also argue that he has a problem with controlling his anger. Maybe he should be sitting here and not me. Maybe I should be sat in his chair right now and him in this one, facing you and talking about anger management.'

'Hmmm,' he says as he writes some notes.

'Don't you find it ironic?' I ask and he looks up. It's clear that he isn't going to answer and wants me to continue with this waffling. He finds it interesting even if I don't so I humour him. 'He has ended up with a job I should have had and I end up in the nuthouse. He punches me in the face, in front of a pub full of people, and it's me who gets criticised at work. It's all very strange.'

'You sound bitter about it.'

'That's probably because I am. That place is run by a bunch of retarded morons.'

'Okay,' he says. 'Maybe it was a good idea then. For you to move on. Have you ever thought about that?'

'Many times. But I had a good job there. I could do it very well, but my face didn't fit in the end. I should be glad I'm out of it.'

He looks at me again. Strangely. Oddly. I can't work out what he's thinking but then, I suppose, it's not my job. It's his. He's supposed to work out what I'm thinking and not the other way around. That's why they pay him the big bucks. That's why he can afford to swan off to the Maldives with his brand new wife and even newer shiny teeth. I wonder if he takes them out each night and puts them in a glass at the side of his bed or if they are screwed into his jaw bone. I ponder this for a few moments because it's infinitely more enjoyable than all this other bullshit.

'We need to get to the bottom of why you did what you did, Alex,' he says, changing the direction of the conversation. 'We need to find out why you have behaved in the way you have. You say you have no recollection of the attack on your wife and the other people and that concerns me. There are also other things that seem to have disappeared from your memory. It's as though your subconscious has blocked it all out, not registering it with your brain.'

I let him talk. I can't be arsed with arguing with him. At this moment all I want to do is to get back to my white bed in my white room.

'And you also haven't yet acknowledged that what you did to Agnes Carter was wrong, have you? Until you can recognise that your behaviour has been, how can I call it, not quite normal, then we cannot make the progress that we need to. At the moment you are a danger to yourself and others. You are unpredictable. You could blow up at any time, without warning.

'I have it here that you managed to upset Eddie and Charlie in the group therapy session with Doctor Green the other day. You don't seem to care how much you offend people.'

'And that's a crime?' I ask. Just what the bloody hell is this man going on about? 'If my words upset people then so what? Lots of people upset lots of other people every day but they don't lock them up for it. I don't care if I upset Scabby Eddie and his dwarf looking friend. I really don't. I couldn't care less. Those people mean nothing to me. Nothing at all. So why should I care about offending them or upsetting them when I don't even care if they exist or not? This is all a load of old shite and I want to go back to my room so you can fill me full of pills and let me sleep.'

'All in good time,' he says calmly. 'All in good time.'

And then he looks at me.

Directly into my eyes.

'Now tell me about Agnes Carter.'

I swallow involuntarily and suddenly feel quite hot and sweaty.

CHAPTER B3
Jenny Sumner

I think about Agnes Carter as I drive home, clutching the ball of tissue to my very sore nose which is still bleeding from Jerry red-nose-fat-bastard's right jab. I occasionally have to leave the tissue hanging from my face whilst I change gear, totally aware that I must look like a total twat. I stop at traffic lights and see other road users, and some pedestrians for that matter, look at me with amusement and it takes every effort to stop myself from ramming the bastards with my much too expensive Ford Focus.

Agnes Carter. Literary agent. My one hope out of the mess that my life is fast becoming. I know she will like what she reads, I just know it. My book is brilliant and I'm not just saying that because it's me. It's because it truly is the best thing I've ever read in many a year. And all from my own hand. God I am talented. I just wish that other people could see it too.

I chose Agnes because she has had many books published that are similar to, but not as good as, mine, and brought success to the authors on her list. I want the same and I deserve it. Then I can walk back into that bloody office and tell all those knobheads who work there to piss off and stick their job up their arses. I can't wait for that day to happen. I long for it. The very thought of it is enough to cheer me up.

I turn onto the main road that leads to my estate and see a familiar car coming in the opposite direction. It's John Michaelson's black BMW and I take my hand from my tissued schnoz and flash my lights at him in greeting. He notices at the last minute and looks at me in shock as he continues past. I manage a laugh to myself. What must I have looked like?

I turn right, onto the estate, and as I pass the Lego looking houses with their well manicured and somewhat ostentatious lawns (if gardens can be ostentatious), I see Jenny's car parked on the driveway of our modest semi-detached house. I pull up next to it and get out. As I fumble for my house key the front door opens and she stands there in the doorway and takes a look at me. My beautiful Jenny. She looks all sweaty and red-faced. It's clear that she has not showered at the gym after her aerobic session, probably waiting to get home to do it, as she often does.

'You been back long?' I ask but she is too flabbergasted at my appearance to answer immediately. 'You look like you've had a good workout.'

'I have,' she says not really registering what I've said. 'What the bloody hell has happened to you? Your face...'

'Oh, don't worry about it,' I say, stepping past her and into the hallway. 'Just a little misunderstanding in the pub after work. I think I upset someone.'

'Clearly,' she says following me as I walk upstairs to the bathroom. 'What have you done now?'

'What do you mean "now"?' I ask as I run the tap in the bathroom sink, scooping water into my face to wash away the blood that has dried there.

'Come on, Alex,' she says. 'You've been a pain in the arse recently and you know it. You don't seem to consider anyone's feelings in anything you do. I'm not surprised that someone has given you a wallop. Who was it?'

'Thanks for the support,' I say sarcastically. 'Bit much to ask, eh? A little support from my wife? And how do you know that it was all my own fault?'

'Just an educated guess,' she says. She knows me too well!

'I might have been a little bit out of order, if I'm honest,' I concede, attempting a smile through the mirror as I continue to wipe away the dried blood from my mush. 'I've had a bad day though, love. It looks like I might be getting laid off. I will be getting laid off if that cow Felicity

Henderson has anything to do with it. I hate her and she hates me.'

'I know, Alex, you tell me every day.'

'Sorry if I'm boring you with it.'

'Can't you just try to get on with these people?' she says almost desperately. 'We've got a mortgage and two cars to pay for. We can't afford for you to lose your job.'

'I might not have too much choice in the matter,' I reply, towelling my face. 'For some reason I can't hold my tongue with her... or the other morons who are in charge there at the minute. It used to be a great job until they took over. Now it's just shit.'

'Well look for another one then.'

'I won't have them force me out,' I reply, looking into her beautiful green eyes. 'I've been there for years and am good at what I do. They've been there for five minutes and are shit at what they do. It's them who should be leaving, not me. They've ruined the place.'

'It doesn't work that way, Alex, and you know it,' she responds. Quite correctly I'm sorry to say. I know that I'm probably flogging a dead horse where work is concerned. If they are prepared to give Jerry a promotion and let me go, then it's clearly obvious that the place is going to the dogs. Better to take the money, whatever pittance they are prepared to offer, and run. I'm sure that with my experience and talents that I won't be out of work for long. And then there's always my fledgling writing career too. When that takes off then work is one stress that will immediately disappear.

I walk into the bedroom to shower and see that the bed hasn't been made since this morning and I pull the duvet over to straighten it out. It's not like Jenny to leave it in such a mess (I'm usually up for work an hour before she is) but I won't say anything as I am already in her bad books enough and don't wish to antagonise her any further. I go back into the bathroom and turn on the shower, feeling the water with my hand until it gets warm enough.

A half hour later, suitably cleaned and refreshed, I go downstairs to find Jenny sitting in front of the television, watching one of those soaps and eating a microwave pasta meal straight from the plastic packaging. Saves on washing up, she says. She does not look up as I enter the room, clearly more interested in the fictional soap opera on screen than in the very real soap opera that my life is fast becoming.

I leave her to it.

Eventually, during the advertisement break she turns to look at me. 'Aren't you having anything to eat?' she asks, then turns her head back to watch the very rich David Beckham earning some more well deserved money advertising for Sky Sports. Like he really could do with the money. I feel for him, the poor sod.

'I've lost my appetite,' I reply.

I'm expecting her to say something to break my indifferent attitude towards eating and keeping healthy, being my wife and that, but instead she just mumbles, 'Okay. Suit yourself.'

I observe her for a while, sitting there watching the crap that modern TV spews out to the masses. Some "not right" on the TV tells us that there is a show on later that we should not miss, and if we do, then we can always get it on "Catch-Up". It's about gardening, or cooking, or some other such bollocks and I think to myself that I will definitely not be watching it. Not at the time it's aired, not on the plus one channel and most definitely not on bloody Catch-Up. Thanks, but no thanks! Thanks for making me aware which bloody channel not to be watching later.

After a while, when the programme has finished, she stands up and goes to the kitchen to make a cup of tea. She returns and sits down, seemingly oblivious to me actually being in her company.

I wonder what is becoming of us. There was a time, not that long ago too, where she would actually look pleased to see me, unable to keep her hands off me, sometimes in the most inappropriate of places (I mean geographically, not physically!), but now, for the last few months, she has been distant. Whenever I broach the subject she says she doesn't know what I'm on about and there's nothing wrong, but I'm not so sure. Maybe I've spent too much time in the study writing the book. Maybe I've neglected her a little. Whatever it is, she won't talk about it.

'So what are your options?' she suddenly says, taking me by surprise.

'My options?' I'm not quite sure what she means.

'Yeah, your options,' she says as though I'm an idiot. 'With work.'

'Oh, right,' I reply. 'I'm not sure yet. I suppose they'll have me in to discuss it but it looks like they want me out. Apparently that Jerry bloke is getting promoted and I'm sure it's into my job, but they won't admit that.'

'So why would they do that? It doesn't make sense.'

'Like I keep telling you. The place is run by a bunch of idiots at the minute and, to be honest, I'm not sure that I want to work for those people anymore.'

'Well don't make any rash decisions without speaking to me first,' she says sternly. God forbid if I was ever to do anything on my own initiative!

'Right, love,' I reply robotically. 'Anyway, when my book is taken up then neither of us will have to work.'

'Don't pin all your hopes on that,' she says seriously. 'It might not be what they are looking for.'

Not to be put off by her pessimism, I reply. 'It's bloody good, Jen. It's a matter of time that's all. The agent I've sent it too will love it, believe me.'

'Well don't build your hopes up too much. That's all I'm saying, Alex. It will just make the disappointment of rejection that much worse.' She jumps up. 'Time for a shower,' she says and leaves the room.

I sit there in silence for a few minutes, my thoughts wandering. The television spews out the next load of shite but I am oblivious to it, the sound merely white noise in the background. I can't understand Jenny's lack of enthusiasm and encouragement for my project. It's taken me months to write, almost a year, and she's read it and said she enjoyed it. So it must be good. Or was she just saying that because she's my wife?

Anyway, Agnes Carter will be in touch soon. I'm just waiting for my phone to ring or for that email from her asking for the full manuscript.

It's just a question of time.

Why have Depeche Mode suddenly come into my head?

I go to the CD rack to search for their Greatest Hits.

Listening to eighties electropop has got to be better than watching bloody Masterchef.

#

I enter the bedroom, the lyrics to "Enjoy the Silence" running around my head and in the darkness I can just make out Jenny in the bed.

I can see that she is either already asleep or pretending to be, I can't quite tell. I creep around the bed, careful not to bang my shins against the wooden frame, which I tend to do from time to time, and drop my clothes onto the floor as I take them off. I can't be bothered to go to the bathroom to clean my teeth as I know that the chances of getting a goodnight kiss off her are pretty much zero, so why bother? The chances of ever getting a kiss off her these days, goodnight or not, are about the same.

I slip under the duvet and edge towards her, the heat of her body a marked contrast against the coldness of the sheet and she moves away instinctively. I try to get a little nearer but she just moves away further.

'Jen,' I whisper. 'Are you awake?'

She doesn't reply. 'Jen, Jen. Are you awake?' I repeat.

'Bloody hell, Alex!' she replies, turning onto her back. 'If I wasn't then I am now. Thanks.'

'Sorry,' I say sheepishly.

'What do you want?' I can tell that I've pissed her off. Again.

'Nothing,' I say. 'I just thought that you might want a chat or something.'

'What I want to do is sleep,' she replies. 'I'm knackered. I've had a busy day.'

'Me too,' I respond. 'I've had a totally shit day and I just thought that you might want to offer me some kind of sympathy or something.'

'Alex, don't you think that sometimes some of your problems are of your own making? I don't know why you can't just knuckle down sometimes and just get on with it. Most people don't like their jobs but most people just get on with them 'cos they pay the bills. That's all there is to it.'

I sigh. I suppose a bit of sympathy from my wife was a little too much to ask.

'Maybe I need a holiday,' I say.

'Maybe you do. That's the first sensible thing that you've said in a while. Why don't you get some brochures tomorrow, during your dinner break.'

At last. I smile to myself, things aren't so bad between us after all. 'Okay,' I say, 'Where do you fancy going?'

'Oh, I won't be coming with you,' she responds quickly. 'I've much too much to do here. And I won't get the time off work anyway. You'll have to go on your own. Or take a friend or something.'

'For God's sake, Jenny. Is it too much for you to spend a bit of time with me.'

She ignores me. 'Alex, I'm tired. I need to sleep. I think you going away for a bit will do you good. I think it's a great idea. Recharge your batteries and all that.'

I don't reply. I don't want to reply. I don't want to go away on my own. She may think it's a good idea. I think it's a totally shit idea.

Although my nostrils are blocked with dried blood a sweet odour suddenly makes it's way through and I try and sniff a little harder to see what it is. This just forces mucus and blood to the back of my throat and I cough and hawk loudly to prevent myself from choking on it. I jump out of bed quickly and head to the en-suite.

'Jesus, Alex, that's disgusting!' shouts Jenny.

I get to the bathroom and spit the bloody contents of my mouth into the toilet and after wiping my mouth with some toilet roll, I flush it away.

'Sorry, Jenny,' I say apologetically. 'That was disgusting, yes, but I couldn't help it. Some prick punched me in the face earlier, remember. I think my nose might be broken.'

'Well if you're going to snore tonight you can sleep in the other room.' Bloody hell, the sympathetic cow!

'What's that smell?' I ask, remembering the reason for my new sudden bout of discomfort.

'What do you mean?' she asks quietly.

'On the bed. I smelled something sweet. That's why I sniffed up all this bloody snot and gunk.'

I hear her move and can tell she is sniffing the bedclothes.

'Erm… Oh yes,' she says, suddenly remembering. 'I spilled some perfume on the bed this morning when I was getting ready. I'll wash it all in the morning.'

'Right,' I say. My head is now banging with pain and I can't seem to think straight. Maybe she is right and it's best for me to sleep in the spare room tonight. The last thing I want to do is to keep her awake and antagonise her any further. There's enough shit going on in my life right now without me and the wife arguing.

I clean my teeth to take away the sweet taste of blood and snot from my mouth and as I head for the sanctuary of the spare room I notice that Jenny has fallen asleep.

Or has pretended to. I'm not too sure.

CHAPTER A4
The Quiet One

'You were going to tell me about Agnes Carter,' says Mister Andrews looking up from his notes.

'Was I...? Do I have to?' I answer. I am somehow not able to look at him. This is a subject that I really don't want to talk about.

'Eventually you will have to,' he replies calmly. Almost nicely. As though being nice to me will coax me to speak about things that I would sooner forget. 'If you want to get out of here then you will have to face up to everything that you've done that has put you in here. Until you face these things how can you deal with them?'

'By forgetting about them,' I proffer. But I know that he won't accept an answer like that.

'It doesn't work that way, Alex,' he says. 'And you know it. You seem an intelligent man. Some might think too intelligent. But you don't seem to know, or are in any way concerned, about how your actions affect other people. You need to control that or you will always have problems.'

'I used to be the quiet one,' I tell him. 'I used to be the one who would let things go... let people think that they were better than me if that's what they wanted to think. But then suddenly it hit me that I didn't have to put up with all that bullshit if I didn't want to. I didn't have to be quiet Alex who said nothing when others were being arseholes. So I started to tell them what I thought. I've suffered fools enough in my lifetime and I've made a promise to myself that I'll suffer them no more. You included.'

He looks up again, at me, but does not respond to my remark, choosing to pretend that he didn't hear it.

'Agnes Carter,' he persists. 'What happened with Agnes Carter?'

'I got sidetracked a little,' I confess. 'I thought that I knew something that she didn't and it got a little out of control. I have apologised already for this.'

'You left the poor girl severely traumatised.'

'I know,' I answer meekly. Because I can't respond to that particular issue any other way.

He looks at me as though he knows something I don't, but I don't pursue it. I don't want to pursue it because pursuing it means that I have to talk about it and I'm not quite ready for that just yet. I made a total idiot of myself and I want to just leave it at that. I accept it. It happened and I am more than a little bit embarrassed by it. So there you are. That's it. No more.

'Are you still waking up in tears?' he asks and I thank God to myself that he has changed the subject.

'Yes, I am,' I reply.

For it is the truth.

CHAPTER B4
You Can Never Win An Argument With A Stupid Person

My eyes are beginning to blacken as I walk into the office the next morning and my nose is very bloody sore, making it quite difficult to breathe. Thankfully I don't have to pass Jerry red-nose's department and so we can both avoid the awkwardness of having to see or speak to each other for the time being. I am still not sure about who should be apologising to who, but I'm not the one who got violent, so I suppose it should be him apologising to me.

I walk past the few people I am responsible for as they log onto their computers, each of them looking at me and instantly turning away upon seeing the state of my face, and as I enter my small office I can already hear the muted whispers as the story of what happened in the George and Dragon is spread around the workplace.

I find that I don't particularly care. Let them talk. What can they say that can make it any worse. I have now got to motivate myself and my workforce even though I know that I will be out on my ear in a few short weeks. Now that isn't going to be easy.

I log onto my computer and go straight to my emails. There is one from Felicity, sent only five minutes ago, asking me to go and see her at one o'clock. She has used the phrase "moving forward" yet again which she does on every email she ever sends, which gets right on my tits. No imagination some people (or is it lack of intelligence? I'm not too sure).

I sigh. Can I really be bothered with more of her bullshit? They still pay me my wages so I suppose that I had better turn up, no matter how much I would rather not. Maybe John was right last night in the pub and Jenny too, later on. Maybe I do need that holiday. It's persuading

Jenny to come with me that's the awkward thing. She is quite happy for me to go away on my own to recharge my batteries, as she put it, but she is much too busy. Why is she much too busy? She doesn't make sense sometimes. In fact she was a little too enthusiastic for me to get away for a few days. I sigh and make a mental note to check the internet later for short breaks.

I look down the list of emails. Only four new ones. The one from Felicity. Something about jobs workshops from HR (Christ, they didn't waste any time!), one from Liam about his latest whinge which I delete without looking at, and finally one that instantly grabs my attention. This is one that I really should have had sent to my home email account but I had given her my work address so I would get it straight away, not having one of those fancy mobile phones where you can receive your emails and all that.

It's from Agnes Carter, literary agent.

At first I don't want to open it. This is too big a moment for me. This could be the one I've been waiting for, the one that changes my life forever. She has only had my submission for four weeks and must have finally got round to reading it.

Tentatively I hover the cursor over it, at first resisting clicking the mouse to open it, but I cannot hold back for very long and press down on the button.

Dear Alex
Many thanks for your submission
This is not something for me but I want to wish you all the best in your search for representation
Kind Regards
Agnes

That's it...?
That's it?
That's the response I get after a year's worth of work and effort? Slaving over a laptop for hours on end to

produce a literary masterpiece. All shot down to shit with two lines of email text.

Two lines.

Twenty five words.

Seventy nine characters, (not including the meaningless pleasantries!).

I know it sounds sad but I've counted them. One hundred percent effort from me, nought percent effort from her. Has she even read it? Well, has she? She couldn't have. Not in such a short space of time. And if she'd read it she would have rang me begging me to give her the full manuscript and to not show it to anyone else. She would have done. Of course she would. My novel is brilliant.

I sit back in the chair, completely lost for words. Okay the book is out with other agents too, but it was Agnes Carter I wanted. She is the perfect agent for this type of material. How can it be "not something for me"? It just doesn't make sense. Of course it's something for her. It's something for everyone, surely. She wishes me "all the best in your search for representation". Yeah right. Of course she does. It's a bog-standard message. A template, so she doesn't even have to type out the two lines, twenty five words or seventy nine characters. The computer will do that for her. And it's not even punctuated!

I put my elbows on the desk and put my head in my hands. I'm aware of those outside the office looking in at me and so I get up and close the blinds. I need to be alone. This is dreadful news. The worst ever. After all that is happening to me, I just cannot believe it. It's just one thing after another.

After a while there is a knock at the door and Steve Murphy, one of the clerks, looks in, with what appears to be a hint of concern on his face. 'You okay, boss?' he asks.

I take my head from my hands and reply. 'Yes. Why wouldn't I be?'

'It's just that you yelled out a few moments ago and I wanted to see if you were all right.'

'Thanks for your concern, Steve, but I'm okay. Honestly.'

He nods and realises that to carry on with the conversation would be futile and so he leaves, shutting the door behind him.

Did I really shout out? That's a bit strange because I can't remember doing so. Jesus! What is happening to me?

Eventually, I stand up and pull up all the blinds and then go and open the door. I don't want the staff thinking I'm going crazy or something, and maybe if they can see me, in my office and working as normal, then they will see that I'm okay.

But am I though? I'm not even too sure myself. Okay, I'm under a lot of stress at the moment, what with Jenny seemingly indifferent to me, my job under threat, being punched by a red-nosed fat, useless git and now my novel being rejected. I know I have been speaking my mind a bit lately, probably a little disrespectfully too, if I'm being honest, but that doesn't mean that I'm losing it, surely. I'm not going mad. No way. Well not just yet anyway. However I must have shouted out without realising it because I can't see Steve lying about it. Why would he? I make a conscious mental note to make sure that I think before I act in future. If I can. But working in this place is going to make that particular promise to myself very difficult to keep.

As dinner time approaches I decide that I will go to the canteen with the others. I was going to hide away in my office, just me and my bruises, but now it has come to it, I think it best that I front it out and show my somewhat battered face to the rest of the building. So what? I'm sure the story, in all its embellished forms, has spread around the place like a Californian forest fire. I don't rightly care anymore. Let them think and say what they want.

I enter the spotless canteen. It is basically the typical, sterile type of room, seen up and down the country in thousands of workplaces just like this one. Polished wooden tables with "stylish" plastic chairs, a serving area where you can purchase salads, soups, sandwiches and a choice of two or three hot meals all at so-called subsidised prices, served by cooks who dish out the slop as though it's of five star hotel quality, when in fact it is more to the standard of a Victorian workhouse. But God forbid if you wanted to make a complaint. Then you would suffer the wrath of the canteen staff, no matter how high up the chain you happened to be. I once saw a director make a comment about how his chips were a little on the cold side. It's a wonder he left the place alive! Even I, with my mouth, know to keep quiet in this place.

I see a few of my colleagues sitting at a table in the corner and so I walk over and sit with them. Steve is there along with Helen Jones (I've heard the odd rumour that they had a bit of a fling on the last Christmas do, but that's all I know. I don't go for that kind of tittle tattle). Liam Morris sits opposite them next to Derek Shuttleworth.

Derek is one of those guys who seems to float through life as though it's all a game and why he is employed here is beyond me, because he certainly has no interest in the job. I'm guessing, if they have any sense, (which they are yet to show) that they are going to use this restructuring to get rid of guys like him. But then what do I know? They'll probably promote him instead.

'Hi, boss,' says Steve pleasantly. He looks at my blackening eyes but pretends not to notice, maybe feeling discretion is in order. Or is it embarrassment? 'Get up to anything last night?' His attempts at small talk cause the others to cringe slightly at his tactless question.

I decide to lighten the moment. 'Yes, mate,' I reply. 'I had a couple of pints after work and got twatted in the face by old red nose.'

There is an awkward silence. They don't know whether to laugh or not.

'Did you deserve it?' asks Liam boldly.

'I suppose so,' I reply. 'I was taking the piss a bit and he over-reacted a little. You see, the thing is, you can never win an argument with a stupid person, because the stupid person isn't aware that they are stupid and therefore always think that they're right and clever, even when they're clearly not. And that's because they're stupid. And the ironic thing is they in turn think that you are stupid, because they don't understand you. So to prevent conflict, the clever person has to pretend that they are the stupid one to avoid getting a punch in the face. I just wasn't prepared to do that last night and that's why my face looks like this today. Learn the lesson people, learn the lesson. So let's leave it at that shall we. Anyway what's going on with you lot?'

Liam looks a little uncomfortable. 'I've had a date through for my hearing,' he says. 'You know, the one you told me not to waste your time with.'

'I told you not to waste my time with it, because that's exactly what it is. A total waste of time and not to mention, totally trivial,' I respond. I can't believe the lad actually went above my head with this. He looks at me a little embarrassed but if he wants to bring this up in front of the others then I've no problem with telling him what I think about it.

'Well anyway,' he says sheepishly. 'I think I have a point and so do a lot of other people.'

'They're just humouring you,' I say. 'They're just being nice to you. You could make yourself look like a fool over this. It's a bloody badge, Liam. It's meaningless. In the whole scheme of things, it's a joke. What's written on your bloody badge is not important.'

I can see he is affronted and despite me technically being his boss (or line manager being the twenty first century term) he is not afraid to argue with me over the matter. I can see the other three squirming in their chairs, well Steve and Helen anyway, Derek seems more interested in the cricket report in the newspaper he is reading and looks oblivious to all else around him, including this conversation, which is typical of him.

'I have a point,' Liam persists. 'When I need to go into other departments they'll think I'm just an office clerk.'

'You are just an office clerk.'

'No I'm not, I'm an Admin Co-ordinator.'

'Which is just a fancy name for an office clerk,' I tell him. 'It's a made up title for a bullshit job. There's loads in this place. Have you seen all the new positions on the intranet and in the company telephone directory? Apparently we now have a "Corporate Strategy Consultant" and an "Inter-departmental Liaison Officer". Have you any idea what those people do or how much they get paid for doing it, whatever it is? No? Neither do I. And more worryingly, neither do they. They're made up bullshit titles for made up bullshit jobs to make the company look more modern and corporate. It's total crap.'

His face is reddening but I don't care. In fact I don't care one bit.

'There are people here, some probably sat around this table, who face the prospect of redundancy,' I go on. 'You've all heard the rumours. And all you care about is what's written on your bloody badge. Get a grip, my friend, before someone gets a grip of you, and to use a word that landed me in lumber yesterday... literally! If you spent as much time concentrating on your work than actually bloody moaning about it, then you might get more done and actually have less to whinge about. Have you ever thought about that?'

He stands up, his face now very red to match his very red hair and if I'm not mistaken he has tears in his eyes. He walks away quickly.

'Do you think that was a bit harsh?' I say to the others after a while.

Derek looks up from the paper. 'Sorry boss... was what too harsh?'

'Maybe a little,' says Steve. 'You know how sensitive he can get. But more importantly, what's all this about redundancies? Has something been confirmed?'

Oops! Maybe I shouldn't have mentioned that. But hell, these people should know if their jobs are under threat. They shouldn't be kept in the dark.

'I expect there to be an announcement soon,' I say. 'I'm sorry but I can't tell you any more than that. To be honest, I don't know any more than that myself.'

At five to one I make my way to the top floor. Passing Annette Foster at her computer, playing Solitaire and eating some kind of fancy sandwich, I walk to Felicity's office and knock firmly on the door. The blinds on the windows and door are down and I am unable to see inside, and so, when I enter the room I do not realise that fat Jerry red-nose and the big chief himself, the managing director of the company, Sid McGuigan, are also in the room. Felicity and Jerry sit either side of him at a table facing me. There is a single chair on the opposite side of the desk, facing them, which I suppose has been put there for me to sit on, as though for a job interview or something. For some reason, this does not feel right. It feels like a court martial.

None of them stand as I walk in and they are all looking down at various pieces of paper that lie on the table in front of them. As I walk towards them, McGuigan says, without looking up, 'Please sit down,' and so, like the good boy that they want me to be, I place my arse on the chair.

McGuigan is another of those who are in a job beyond their capabilities. The guy is only interested in making "efficiency savings" and has no thought for the quality of the service we are providing as a company. I have no doubt that this will come back to haunt him eventually. He offers words of wisdom via his infernal intranet blog, which are all a load of old bollocks and completely condescending. He has the uncanny ability to patronise people to the point where they would sooner stab him in the head with a rusty nail than say hello to him, which, in my opinion, would be the best career move anyone could make if they actually did it. He is a tall skinny guy and because I hate him with a passion, even his whiny little voice grates me to the point of torture. However, he is my boss (for the time being) and so I had better show him the respect the role requires. Respect to the role that is and not to him personally. Let's get that straight. I have absolutely no respect for him as a person. None whatsoever. He's a twat.

Finally he looks up. I'm alarmed to see that he is not smiling that smug bastard smile he has down to a tee. Which concerns me greatly as I settle into my seat.

'Do you know why you are here?' he asks.

'No,' I reply.

'Then I will get to the point,' he says firmly. 'In the past twenty four hours you have managed to upset both of these good folks. Your attitude and actions have not been in compliance with company policy of anyone employed by this organisation.'

'Whoa, whoa, whoa,' I say, raising my right hand. 'With respect, Mr McGuigan. If this is some kind of disciplinary hearing then I should have been informed as such and should have been allowed to bring in a union rep.'

'This is an informal meeting,' he says. 'There is no need to involve the union.'

'I'll be the judge of that,' I reply. 'I was asked to come to a meeting with Felicity. I didn't know that you were going to be here and I didn't know that it was about my behaviour. Had I known that, then I would not be sitting here right now. There are policies and procedures to follow, written by your department, Felicity,' I say looking at her. She looks back at me blankly through her idiotic spectacles and once again all I can think of is Dustin Hoffman. 'An informal first stage disciplinary matter doesn't usually warrant the attendance of the managing director.'

It is apparent that the other two are there to provide back up to McGuigan. He is too much of a wet lettuce who lacks the intelligence to argue with someone who is clearly a lot cleverer than he is. One thing I have learned working here: it's not always the most intelligent that get to the higher positions. As long as you can kiss the right arses (especially McGuigan's) and put your knives into the right backs (for example, mine), then you will go far, my son!

'This is not a disciplinary matter… '

'Good. Can you put that in writing?'

'Like I said, this is an informal… chat.'

I decide to hear him out. Let's see what the prick has to say.

'We are a little worried about you,' he says in that condescending, patronising manner that I mentioned earlier. 'Your behaviour has left a lot to be desired recently. You seem to have developed a lack of respect for authority.'

'I just say things as I see them,' I reply. I have nothing to apologise for and I am not going to apologise to these three morons.

'Well maybe sometimes you need to hold your tongue,' he continues. 'I will not have you swearing at Felicity or any other folks for that matter.' (Folks? Who does he think he is? George 'Dubya' Bush?)

I will not apologise, I swear I will not apologise.

'Sorry about that,' I say.

Damn!

'It's not just that,' he condescendingly continues, looking down at me from his elevated seating position, as though he is a monarch who has to be higher than everyone else, like Yul Brynner in 'The King And I' or someone. 'It's your whole attitude. I understand your work is good, we are not having a go at you for that, it's just that your current behaviour is not what is expected from an employee of this firm. Look at your face for example.'

I sit up straighter. If he wanted to wind me up then he has just succeeded.

'Well that was hardly my fault.' I look at Jerry who avoids my gaze like the snake he is, and turns his attention back to the papers in front of him.

'Yes,' carries on McGuigan, 'Jerry came to me this morning to let me know about the accident in the pub last night.'

I am incensed. Accident! The sneaky little shit.

'If you can say a punch to the nose is an accident then I suppose it was, yes.' I can feel my face getting as red as Jerry's.

'Oh, come on now,' says McGuigan. 'Let's not get melodramatic about it shall we?'

'He's lucky I didn't call the police and have him arrested for assault,' I almost shout. 'And there were plenty of witnesses, believe me. There were loads of other "folks" there!'

McGuigan looks to his right at Jerry who continues to look down at his paperwork. It's clear that McGuigan is not particularly interested and is probably secretly happy that the guy has had a pop at me.

Felicity finally says something. 'Maybe you need a break, Alex. Maybe you're a bit stressed. Maybe it might be best if you take some holidays. I believe you have a few days left. Why don't you take them? It might do you good.'

'What, moving forward?' I ask, but she is too thick to understand my sarcasm. 'Maybe I'm a little concerned that I won't have a job to come back to if I do,' I add.

'That's another thing that we need to discuss,' interjects McGuigan. 'I believe Felicity spoke to you yesterday, before your outburst.' I nod but say nothing. 'Well I can confirm that yours is a department that will be re-structured. I can give you notice now that your department will be merged with Jerry's here and so we need only one person to run it. As Felicity alluded to yesterday, I can confirm that when the merger happens we cannot keep you both on at that level. Jerry here will take over as department head and we will try to find you a redeployment opportunity, but I cannot guarantee that it will be the same grade as you are currently on. In fact I can confirm to you now that it won't be. If you want to take a severance package I'm sure the firm will be very generous.'

I can't believe what I'm hearing. How much worse can this day get? The guy is telling me there is no longer a position for me. Suddenly the words to The Jam's

"Smithers-Jones" enter my head and I have to stop myself from singing them out loud. Here we go again...

'I can't believe this,' I say, although it is something I've been expecting. 'Why him? Why not me? I've been here longer and have a load more experience than him. And you've just told me that my work is good.'

'It is,' he says. 'But let's face it. Experience doesn't really matter in the modern workplace now does it?'

I nearly fall off my chair at the man's complete and utter buffoonery. How the hell did this idiot become the managing director of such a big firm as this? It beggars belief. It really does.

'Experience doesn't matter?' I say, laughing. Yes, I am actually laughing and by the look on the imbecile's face it's clear that he doesn't appreciate my response. I know I need to calm down but I just can't accept all this stupidity. Something in my head won't allow it. 'Experience is everything. For God's sake! it's a complete mystery to me how the hell this firm is still going with people like you three in charge. I give it twelve months before all the "good folks" here are out of work, if that's the kind of thing that you believe. Laughable. Totally laughable.'

Before they have chance to respond I stand up. I look directly at Felicity, who, once again, just like yesterday afternoon, looks totally bemused and shocked that I have the audacity to have an opinion and am willing to express it.

'I will take the holiday I am owed,' I say. 'And I will take it from right now. This minute. I'm going home. I can't stand another second in your company. If you want to speak to me about this or any other matter relating to my employment, attitude and all that other stuff, then please speak to my union representative first. And don't ever con me into attending what is essentially a disciplinary hearing without first giving me prior warning or denying me the right to have someone in here with me. Goodbye.'

I turn and leave the room.

Two minutes later, my head banging and with a face that probably looks like the proverbial thunder, I enter my department and head straight to my office to log off my computer and collect my coat. As I walk through the room I can see everyone staring at me. Steve, who is discussing something with Anthony Speakman, that soft bugger of a line manager of mine, looks up and offers a token, wry smile. I do not smile back.

And then I see Annette Foster approaching, skipping down the corridor like some bibbedy bobbedy Disney bitch, her ponytail swinging from side to side and bouncing off her shoulders as she strides confidently along. I am immediately reminded of a real pony, the back end of which is just like her, with tail swishing and horse shit spouting from it's arse, or in Annette's case, her irritating little mouth.

'Hi, hi, hi,' she sings out as she gets closer, a broad smile stretching across her ugly little face. 'Hi Alex. Are you okay?'

'No I'm not,' I say. 'This place is run by knobheads and imbeciles who are worse than bloody useless.'

'Oh, come on,' she chirrups merrily, that permanent smile fixed to her punchable little face. Stupid bitch! 'Things can't be that bad. Turn that frown upside down. Come on. Think happy thoughts. Happy, happy happy!'

I stop and look at her and say the only thing appropriate for a situation such as this.

'Annette... Fuck off.'

CHAPTER A5
The Visitor

It's Saturday and that means it's visiting day.

Visiting day is always a disappointment to me. It's only ever mother who turns up. Not that I don't appreciate her visits, but it's always the same thing. The usual questions about my health, my state of mind, what have I been doing, what have the doctors said, have I been taking my pills et cetera, et bloody cetera. Father came with her once but I think I upset him and he told me that he wouldn't come again unless I apologised to him, which is something I haven't yet got round to doing. I suppose I will at some point, but not just yet. At least this way I don't have to hear about his latest round of golf or what is happening at the bloody bowling club.

Visiting day is a disappointment because the one person who I want to come never does.

Jenny. Who else?

I can't really blame her after what happened, but then I can hardly be held totally responsible now can I? It wasn't all my fault. Mitigating circumstances. Diminished responsibility. Extreme provocation. Call it what you will. It all had a hand in it somewhere along the line, I'm sure. Not that I'm justifying what I did. Of course not. It's just there were factors that led to what happened that were outside of my personal control. If I have to accept responsibility then others also have to accept their part in it. It cuts both ways.

I wait all morning in my room. I don't want to leave and join in with the others in their morning routines and I sit patiently looking out of my barred windows. From here I can see to the motorway and can hear the familiar sound of traffic as it passes along, taking people about their lives and I am hit with a bout of jealousy. I am cooped up in here on a glorious, sunny day, which, let's face it, in England, even in the summertime are few and far between.

However, today I find that I am quite chilled out. Maybe it's the pills that I take; the nurses have delivered them to me a half hour ago and I took them quietly as they watched (they still don't trust me to spit them out). Maybe this therapy is working because today I feel more relaxed than I have done in a long while. More at peace, so to speak. I have no idea why, but I am grateful for the feeling, however it has reached me.

The clock ticks around and I lie on the bed, reading the latest offering from Jo Nesbo that mother brought in last week. Its his usual thing. Gruesome murders in Norway with an alcoholic policeman on the trail. All good stuff. It takes me away from my situation and I find myself grateful for that.

Dinner time comes around and the girls in white tentatively enter the room with a tray of food. They still look at me nervously, as though I'm about to jump out at them or something, like some kind of serial killer from Nesbo's books, but I find that this time I smile at them and say 'thank you' as they place the tray on my trolley and leave the room. I put the book down and look at today's offering. It looks like chicken but you can never be too sure in this place. I put a piece in my mouth and it tastes like chicken so I suppose it must be. In a mushroom sauce. Not that bad really.

I try to think back at how long I have been here. I can vaguely remember being in a police cell and a doctor coming to see me. I can barely remember what he said or what had happened after I left Agnes Carter in that side street. The bit between leaving her and being in police custody is still a blank to me. Totally. Maybe one day I will remember but it isn't happening just yet.

It gets to five to one and the young pretty nurse comes to the door. 'Visitor for you, Alex,' she says quickly and then shuts the door behind her. Still a little scared of me, I suppose. It makes me feel uneasy that people can actually be frightened of me.

I make my way, along with the others, through the whitewashed, chair-lined corridors, filled with trolleys of medical stuff and the occasional abandoned wheelchair and past the vending machines and games room until I come to the visiting room. Brian or Ryan is standing at the far door, the door that leads to the outside world and freedom. There are other members of staff in the room too, all watching us as we enter the room and I look around in search of a familiar, normal face, someone whose existence proves that there is a life for me beyond these walls.

I see her almost immediately, sitting in the far row. For some reason she is wearing a coat, despite it being almost thirty degrees outside. It has always amused me... no scratch that, not amused... bemused... it has always bemused me why old people have to be red hot all the time. There was a time when Jenny, when we were first married, worked in an old persons' home. She told me that during the summertime they would sit there in jumpers and coats, with the heating on full power and the windows closed. It was stifling but they would moan as soon as a member of staff wanted to open a window to let a little breeze in. Strange people, the old. Very strange.

I walk over and sit down opposite her. She looks at me with a smile and sad eyes. It must break her heart to have to visit me in this place.

'Hiya mum,' I say as I pull the chair into the table. I have to sit right up to the table. Don't ask me why because I don't know, I just feel more comfortable like that.

'Hiya, son,' she says. And then she goes into the usual questions. How are you? Are you eating? Are you taking your pills? Same old, same old.

'I'm fine, mum,' I say. 'Truly I am. I'm sure it won't be long before they let me out of here.'

'What have they said?'

'Well, you know, the usual stuff. That I'm making progress and that.'

It's lies of course, they have said nothing of the sort. But if I don't tell her this then she will worry more and mither me continuously. It's easier to let her think that I am getting better, whatever "better" is.

'Well, that's good,' she says. 'Me and your father have decided to take a trip away for a couple of weeks, so I won't be able to come and see you next week… or the week after that, I'm afraid.'

'That's nice,' I reply disinterested. 'Where are you going?'

'He's booked us to go to Majorca. We fly next Friday.'

'Right. Okay. I hope you have a nice time,' I reply nicely, like a nice son should. 'Why is he not here again? I thought he might have come this week.'

'He's still mad at you, Alex. You said some nasty things last time he came.'

'Well, he was being an arse, mum,' I reply. 'I'm supposed to be ill and all he was concerned about was how it looked to his mates at the bloody bowling club.'

'I know,' she says. 'You know what he's like.'

'Yeah, well,' I can feel myself getting worked up and I notice Brian/Ryan looking over at us. I take a breath and lower my voice. 'I do know what he's like but I shouldn't have to put up with it. If I want to say something to him then he should let me speak without getting on his high horse all the time as though he is the superior one. He is so intolerant.'

As I say this, the irony of my words hit me like Jerry's punch. Am I just like my father? Am I that superior to everyone else. My thoughts and actions over the last few weeks, no, months, has been just that. I have been so intolerant of everyone, not just the halfwits I used to work with. Intolerant of the good people, the normal people, the people who mean well. I never used to be like this. Never.

'Are you okay, son?' she says looking at me with that strange concerned look only mothers have for their offspring.

'Yes,' I reply, shaking my head. 'I'm fine.' And then I change the subject completely. Away from my father and how much I am like him. 'Jenny,' I say. 'Have you seen Jenny?'

'No,' she replies and scowls. 'No I haven't. I saw her mother the other day in Asda and she tried to avoid me, but then realised she couldn't and had to speak to me. She asked after you and I said that you were getting better. I asked after Jenny but she was very reluctant to tell me anything but I heard from Margaret Greenhough that… '

Her voice trails away until she stops talking and she looks down at her fingers for some reason. Anything to avoid looking at me. I believe that she thinks that she's said too much.

'Go on,' I say. 'What have you heard from Mrs Greenhough?'

'Oh, you know how she likes to gossip,' she says awkwardly. 'You can't believe what she says half the time. You have to take it with a pinch of salt.'

'Come on, mum. What did she say?'

I can tell it's taking her all her effort to say the words but I stop talking and stare at her. I won't say anything else now until she tells me, and she knows it. She has to answer.

'Oh, she's just saying that Jenny has had that fella moved in. You know the one… '

'Yes,' I reply. 'I know the one all right.'

'But she may have just been saying it to get on my nerves. She knows I don't like her.'

I look at her and she looks back. We both know it's probably true.

So that's the reason why Jenny has never answered any of my letters. It'll be the reason, along with a million others, why she doesn't want to visit me and has changed her mobile phone number. When I think about it I can't really blame her, but it's hard to take that it's finally over. After all these years of being together, most of them happy… until very recently. Well happy for me anyway, if not her.

Mother looks at me with eyes that are sad for me. I'm not sure if they are just sad at how my life has worked out or sad that I have been the architect of my own downfall. Or is it with pity that she looks at me that way. I'm not too sure but I suddenly no longer have the energy to take her to task about it. I will not be pitied. Not by anyone. But the way I feel at this moment, I really can't be upsetting probably the only ally I have left. My dear old mother.

'Don't worry about me,' I say in an attempt to get that look off her face. 'I'll be fine. Maybe a little longer in here and then maybe they will let me out into the big wide world again. Can you do me a favour?' I ask.

'Of course I can,' she says shuffling in her chair. I can tell she is instantly dreading just what that favour may be. She has no need to worry.

'Can you speak to dad for me? Can you tell him I'm sorry and that I'd like to see him again… when you get back from your holidays?' Well, two allies are better than one.

'Yes of course I can.' She sounds relieved. 'Of course I can do that. He will be so happy that you want to say sorry. I'll make sure that he comes on the next visit.'

We chat about other stuff for a while. Insignificant rubbish that people talk about when they have nothing meaningful to say. About how they are thinking of re-decorating the front room and the fact that their next door neighbour's youngest daughter is pregnant to some half-wit with no job (sounds a bit like me!). Things that don't concern me and that I will forget as soon as she's left, but I humour her and pretend to be interested, all the while wanting to go back to my room and wallow in the knowledge that Jenny has made the break.

Made the break totally, convincingly and finally.

I can't deny that I wasn't expecting it, but it still hurts nevertheless. I can feel a knot in my stomach beginning to form and I know that I will not be able to eat later because of it.

As I sit there, with mother babbling on about the kennels she and dad are putting the dog in while they are away, my mind wanders to other things. Well one thing anyway. Jenny. Just Jenny. I remember back to when we first met and how well we got along together. I remember back to my proposal in Paris and her accepting immediately. I remember back to the wedding and what a fantastic day it had been, which was not that long ago, truth be told. I also remember back to how obsessed I became on writing the book and how obsessed she became on getting fit and going to the gym all the time (or so I thought). I remember back to how we slowly drifted apart without either of us (well me anyway) really noticing.

But most of all I remember back to the day I left work early after being told by that complete tosser McGuigan that my career with the company was effectively over. I remember back to getting home, and now I finally remember what happened once I got there. The thing that my mind has been blanking out ever since it happened.

Oh yes, I remember all that. All of it. As though it was yesterday and it's something that I honestly wish had stayed forgotten.

CHAPTER B5
Toilets

I leave Annette-bloody-Foster standing there, looking as though she is about to burst into tears, which, if I admit it, was exactly the reaction I was hoping for, and go in search of my only friend here, John Michaelson. He works on the second floor and I want to see him to thank him for his support because I have a sneaking feeling that it may be some time before I will be coming back. I fully intend to go to the doctors tomorrow and get a sick note for stress. It shouldn't take much to convince him, because, let's face it, bloody stressed is exactly what I am.

I enter John's office area and see red-nosed Jerry going back into his own office in the far corner of the large open room. He looks over but doesn't acknowledge me, which suits me just fine. I ask one of the girls who works there, a young blonde thing, busy typing away furiously at her computer screen, if she has seen him.

'You've missed him,' she says. 'He took half a days flexitime and went home at dinner. He won't be back until tomorrow morning. Can I take a message for him, Mister Sumner?'

'No, it's fine,' I reply. 'I'll catch him later.' (Oh the irony of those words!).

I leave the building and find my car where I left it only a few short hours ago. I get inside and turn the ignition but I do not drive away straight away. I sit there for a while, with the radio on, an irritating DJ with a "Radio One" voice, playing some inane, crap, modern chart hit that can only appeal to the mindless morons of the new generation. The kind who use the word "like" five times in every sentence and wear their trousers half way down their arses to reveal skid stained underwear to all who happen to look their way. I just don't get it. Or am I just getting old?

As this so-called "music" pounds out of the speakers, the "singer" telling me that he is a "gangsta yo yo yo" and to tell him "where are his dogs at?" (whatever the fuck that means), I feel a pounding in my head beating in time with the bass of this utter drivel. I turn off the radio and reach down to the door where I have a bottle of three day old water in the pocket and take a couple of mouthfuls. It has been in the car that long that it is now quite warm and I nearly spit it out, but force myself to swallow it.

I need to take some paracetamol when I get home and hope that we have some in the cupboard because I really can't be bothered to stop off on the way to pick some up. I just want to get home and lie down for the rest of the afternoon. I feel totally drained. Physically and mentally. And my face is bloody well killing me.

Within the space of a few hours my dreams of becoming the next big novelist have been dashed and I've had it confirmed by the big cheese himself that my career with the firm is over. I've even been passed over for the job I should have had by big, fat, ugly, red-nosed, alcoholic Jerry. Christ, I must be bad if they prefer him to me! But then again, you have to look at the calibre of the people making these decisions. Ex-cleaner Felicity Henderson. What the hell does she know about my job anyway? Absolutely nothing. She was not qualified to make that decision, but Sid McGuigan has given her that authority. What a pair of pricks!

No doubt people will tell me that this may be a blessing in disguise. That maybe this is what my career needed. A complete re-boot. A complete re-think on what I want to do with myself. Maybe it will all turn out for the best. But I've put years into this job. Years. Years that now mean nothing to the idiots who are now running the place and that's probably why it hurts so much.

I put the car into gear and shake my head. I need to clear it for the drive home. I have to concentrate on the road and forget about what's just taken place.

As I drive I try to formulate in my mind how I am going to tell Jenny. How can I tell her? What words am I going to use? I know that she will get upset and it pains me to say it, but it won't be about me and how it's affecting my head. It'll be about how we are going to cope with the loss of my wages. The bills, the mortgage, the cars, the phones, they all need paying, and with what she earns, that's not going to cover it. I will have to find another job and find one soon. Pressure, pressure, pressure.

The traffic is slow and the roads are busy and it is some time before I turn into the cul-de-sac where our semi detached house sits amongst the others, all looking the same. Typical suburbia.

I notice straight away that all is not as it should be. Jenny should still be at work but I see that her car is parked on the driveway. And not only that, there is another parked at the side of it, in my spot, where I normally park my car.

At once my senses are alerted and I feel suddenly very, very sick. I pull up behind the two cars and park across them, effectively blocking either from reversing out. I recognise the second car. I know it very well because I have been in it a few times myself. A sense of understanding hits me and I take another swig from the lukewarm water and swallow hard.

I don't want to get out of the car. I don't want to walk into the house and find what I know awaits me inside. All I want to do is drive on. Drive away somewhere so I don't have to face it. Drive away somewhere and pretend that I still don't know what's going on. To bury my head in the sand like an ostrich and ignore it, try to forget it. That way it won't be happening and I can go on in the same ignorance I've been enjoying up until this point.

But I won't do that. What kind of a man does that anyway? Not a real man that's for sure. I will face it and I will deal with it. I don't know how yet, I will find that out when I go into the house.

I get out of the car, leaving the keys in the ignition. I don't know why I do this, I really don't but it's what I do. I walk purposefully to the front door and try the handle. It is unlocked.

Slowly, I open the door, careful not to make any noise and I creep into the house like a burglar, as though it's me who shouldn't be there. I go into the living room and see a man's jacket on the couch. There is no sign of anyone, not a soul, but I can hear movement upstairs. I slip off my shoes and place them near the front door as I walk back to the hallway and then I move slowly towards the stairs.

I can feel the quality of the stair carpet beneath my feet as I slowly creep upstairs. Like the child-catcher in Chitty Chitty Bang Bang (a bloody awful film by the way), I slowly step up the stairs, careful not to make a sound. I squeeze my toes against the carpet and take a deep breath. I'm aware that this is a life defining moment. This is going to change things forever.

I stop outside the bedroom door and I can hear voices inside. The unmistakeable tones of my wife and those of my so called friend. What ratifies my suspicions totally, what makes me understand that I have not been wrong is the sound of the shower in the en-suite running. There is no reason for it to be running, none at all. There is nothing wrong with it so he can't be helping her out with a plumbing issue… well, you know what I mean!

It all comes to me in a flash. The late nights out without me that I was happy for her to go on. It gave me the time I needed to finish and edit my novel. I thought it would do her good to get out with her friends. Him leaving the pub before anyone else last night and checking on how long I was staying out. Seeing him in his car coming from the direction of my house when I returned home. I realise now that the surprised look on his face wasn't due to the bloody tissue hanging out of my nose, he was just surprised to see me coming home so early. The unmade bed. The "spilled perfume" on the bed. The sneaky bastard. I want to kill him.

I can hear his muffled voice coming from the shower as I throw the door open. Jenny, who is lying on her belly on the bed, dressed in a bathrobe and browsing through one of those shitty women's magazines, looks up in shock. Her mouth hangs open as she sees me, unable to comprehend that I am here and have caught the two of them red-handed.

'So what do you think, babe?' I hear him say.

Babe! Bloody babe!

He is clearly unaware that I am here, in the bedroom.

'It's not what you think,' Jenny says frantically as she scrambles off the bed in an attempt to put herself between me and the en-suite, but she is not quick enough.

'Sorry, Jen,' comes the reply from the shower. 'What did you say?'

I look at her and raise my eyebrows.

She looks very sheepish as I force myself past her, throwing her arms off me as they clutch at my arm in a weak attempt to pull me back. I am a man on a mission and I barge into the en-suite and slide back the door to the shower.

The look on his face is almost comical and had this been happening to someone else and not me, then I would have probably laughed. But it is happening to me and not someone else. This is my life that this man is attempting to steal from me. His hair is plastered to his head and his somewhat over-hairy body is full of soap suds. Soap suds generated from my bloody Lynx Apollo. The cheeky bastard is not only poking my wife, he's bloody cleaning himself up with my bloody toiletries. And it's this sheer cheek that finally makes me crack. To shag my wife is one thing. To steal my bloody shower gel is just taking the piss.

I go to grab him but my hands slip from his wet body. I also slip to the floor and grab the first thing I can get hold of, just as Jenny enters the confined space of the en-suite bathroom. I manage to get to my feet again and knock her with my elbow. She falls back into the bedroom, the dressing gown she is wearing slipping to the side to reveal that she is naked underneath.

'Jesus, Alex!' says John-bloody-dirty-bastard-back-stabbing-Judas-bastard-Michaelson, 'Stop it. Let's go downstairs and talk about this.'

'It's a bit too late for that,' I reply as I hit him with this thing that I have grabbed.

I see that the object I have assaulted him with is the toilet brush and, upon realising this, I start to rub it in his face and mouth, all the while my hands and arms getting soaked as the water still pours from the shower. My shower! He slips and falls on his arse, his legs sticking out of the cubicle which makes it easier to force the brush into his mouth, making him gag and thrash about.

My ire is now in full flow and I can't stop myself. I feel a sense of freedom, almost of release, and all the frustrations of the last couple of days come pouring out and manifest itself into a monster within my head, telling me to carry on, to do it more forcefully and I accept this "devil on my shoulder's" instructions willingly and gleefully. I have him trapped in the shower cubicle and force the brush into his mouth as he opens it to shout out a protest. I am aware of Jenny yelling at me but I ignore her. I sense her coming towards me again from the open doorway. I thrust out my arm, my fist automatically clenched and at first I don't realise that I have actually punched her.

I use my now free and slightly sore hand and turn the dial up to full on the shower and feel the instant rise in temperature as it cascades over the bastard. I feel it sting my arms through my shirt sleeves but I don't care now. I am like a man possessed.

'Go on, you bastard,' I say, 'get those teeth clean,' as I forcibly rub the, come to think about it, quite dirty bog brush, roughly into his face and mouth.

John is now screaming and I am aware of Jenny sobbing to my left. I pull the toilet brush from John's mouth, hit him once over the head with it and then throw it back into the shower cubicle with him. As I turn away I can see that his body is now glowing bright red from where the piping hot water is scalding him and his mouth is bleeding from the rough bristles of the shit stained brush, and I feel a minor sense of justice. Let's face it, he bloody-well deserved it.

I go back into the bedroom, stepping over Jenny as she is lying on the floor near the doorway. She makes an attempt to get up, to take hold of me to stop me from leaving the room and as she kneels up, her head in front of me, the temptation to stick my knee into her face is all consuming. (Apparently, so the doctor's and police would tell me later, this is exactly what I did do, but I don't believe them. It's not in my nature to assault a woman. Even a cheating, lying, deceitful bitch like her! I know that I may have caught her when I was shoving the toilet brush down John's throat, to stop her from stopping me, so to speak, but I know that I wouldn't have stuck my knee in her face, however tempting that was at the time. If I did do it then I have not recollection of doing so. Which is a little more than slightly worrying!).

I suddenly get the feeling that I need to get away. I need to get out of the house and far away from the pair of them. Anywhere will do, I'm not particularly bothered. I race down the stairs and go into the living room. For some reason I find that I want my MacBook. I have a sense that it's going to be some time before I come back here because I feel sick to the stomach about the whole thing. I pick it up off the dining room table and head for the front door, slipping my shoes back on in the process.

I can hear movement upstairs but I ignore it. I don't care about the damage I have just caused. I have absolutely no interest in either of them at this moment, I just want to get out of the house. As I am about to leave the living room I see the keys to John's car on the window sill and grab them. I go outside and slam the door of the house behind me as strongly as I can, which is pretty strong, the state I'm in at the moment.

Using his own car keys, I run them down the front wing of his black BMW creating a deep, long white line on the bodywork. I'm aware that this is a childish thing to do but I don't rightly care, it feels good to me. I might as well add criminal damage to the assault charge he may have me done for.

And then another idea crosses my mind. If I am to be done for criminal damage then, hey, in for a penny and all that.

I press the unlock button on his key fob and walk around to the driver's side of the car. I place the MacBook on the roof and open the car door. I then unzip my flies and proceed to pee all over his car seat and find that I am actually laughing as I do so, letting the steaming urine pour out onto the leather, sitting in a pool where the seat dips down slightly. I move around letting it splash into the carpet at the footwell too.

I can hear them both banging on the upstairs bedroom window and their muffled shouts but I don't bother to look up until I've finished and zipped my fly back up. I look at them and can see the disgust on their faces but I just laugh and flick up my middle finger at them both. Taking the MacBook from the roof of the car I walk casually down to my own and open the door.

I get inside and turn the ignition. Putting the car into gear I set off up the street to turn round so I can get out of the cul-de-sac. I have no idea what I'm going to do next. No idea whatsoever. All I want to do at this moment is get as far away from them as I possibly can and to figure out what I am to do next. To work out what my options are.

As I come back up the street, I notice old man Arthur from next door. He is outside and trimming the hedges in his garden and he is looking at me as though I'm some sort of weirdo. It is then I realise that he must have seen everything. He must have seen me scratch John's car and he must also have seen me using it as a toilet. I merely smile and wave at him as I pass and, comically, he rises his hand slightly in greeting, all the time his face looking shocked and bemused.

I drive out of the estate and onto the main road. Realising I still have the keys to his car, which I have thrown onto my passenger seat, I wind down the window and throw them out onto the road.

I have no idea where I'm going. No idea about where I'm going or what I am to do. I can't believe what has happened to me today. This has got to be the worst day I have ever lived and that takes some doing with the shitty days I've had to endure over the past few weeks.

As I drive aimlessly around the streets and roads that are so familiar to me, my mind wanders and a million thoughts hit me at once. Everything arrives in my brain in a jumbled up, mixed up way and I find it hard to arrange them into some kind of order. It makes my head hurt and I pull over to the side of the road to clear it, to shake it so all my thoughts can fall into place.

I think about the imbecilic managers at work and how they have shit on me. I think about Agnes Carter and her off-hand, blasé rejection of months of hard work and how she has shit on me. I think of my one-time friend John Michaelson and how he has been at it with my wife. Again someone who has shit on me. But most of all I think of my beautiful wife, Jenny, and how she has committed the ultimate betrayal and totally, totally, shit on me. Everyone is shitting on me. Why me? What have I done so bad to all these people that they think they can shit on me and keep on shitting on me? Am I that bad a person? I know I can be cutting sometimes and can probably offend people, but did I deserve this? Any of it? Really?

I work myself up to a fury. I need to fight back. Okay, so John Michaelson has just felt my wrath and probably Jenny too, for that matter, but what about the rest? Do they know that they have affected me in such a way that my life has become one complete and utter sewer, one great big pile of crap with each of them adding a bit of shit to it until I need United Utilities or Dynarod or someone to come and clear it up, to unblock all this mess.

I know none of this is my fault. None of it. I did not deserve this.

I put the car into gear again and pull out into the traffic. Immediately I slam on the breaks as a silver Ford I have not seen, beeps its horn as it swerves to avoid me. I raise my hand in apology as the driver, a middle aged bloke in a suit, shakes his head and mouths the word "Wanker" at me. I turn my wave of apology into a two fingered gesture on seeing this and he merely shakes his head and continues driving. I half hope that he will stop and get out so I can beat the living shite out of him, but after a few seconds and a few deep breaths, the feeling of committing strong violence on a complete stranger subsides.

I find myself heading back to work and before I know it I have pulled into the car park and parked back in the spot that I vacated not too long ago. I am not sure why I have come back. I suppose it may be because I don't know where else to go. I could go round to my parents house but I can't be bothered with them just yet, although I know that that is where I will probably have to stay tonight. I have nowhere and no-one else.

I walk determinedly to the entrance and through reception to the lift. Eileen, the receptionist, looks at me oddly as I stand waiting for it to come down to me. I must look a right sight, I imagine, and as I enter the empty lift a few seconds later I am able to take a look at myself in the mirror that immediately faces me inside. I do look a mess. A total bloody mess.

My eyes are now fully black from the wallop that fat bastard Jerry planted on me yesterday and my wet shirt is hanging out of the side and the back of my trousers, after the one-sided scuffle I've just had with John Michaelson. I tuck the shirt in and then press the button for the fourth floor which is at the very top of the building. As the doors close behind me I can see Eileen in the mirror, leaning out over her desk to get a better look at me until the doors close and she vanishes from my view.

It is the fourth floor where all the big bosses work. If you can call it work. I call it destroying peoples lives. It's from the fourth floor that they can pour down their shit onto the real workers, the one's who make them all their profit and provide them with their oversized, unworthy bonuses each quarter. It's like they make these bad decisions from up there and let gravity take over, letting them wash over the rest of us like that very hot shower water has just washed over Michaelson's hairy, scrawny and now very red, body. The very thought of it makes me want to vomit.

I see the lights on the display change from 1 to 2, then 2 to 3, until eventually it stops and the mechanical announcement tells me something I already know 'Fourth floor, fourth floor'. Why it has to tell me twice I do not know, but it does, and as the doors slide smoothly open, I step out into the fourth floor reception area, looking ever so slightly more presentable than I did when I stepped in on the ground floor.

The place looks deserted but I see Annette Foster at her desk with her back to me. I can see from where I'm standing that she is playing Solitaire on her computer. So much for the hard-working office manager then, eh?

She senses my presence behind her and quickly clicks on her mouse to minimise the game, making it disappear from her screen. She turns around with that fake smile on her lips until she sees that it's me and instantly wipes it from her face. She has clearly fallen out with me following my little outburst earlier.

Some people have no sense of humour!

'What do you want?' she asks sternly. 'I thought you'd gone home on leave or something.'

'I had,' I reply. 'But I couldn't keep away from you so I just had to rush back.'

She is so thick that she can't work out if I'm joking or not. But let's face it, you don't have to be clever in this world to get on, you just need not be totally thick. And this girl is very close to 'totally'.

Realising that I am taking the piss, she becomes more serious. 'What is it you want, Alex?'

'I need to see McGuigan.'

'Well you can't,' she replies. 'He's gone for a late lunch with a few of the others. There's only me here right now.'

'So why weren't you invited?' I ask. 'I thought you were really important here. Office manager and all that.'

'Well someone has to be here to do the work,' she replies. She seems affronted by my line of questioning which I find hilarious.

'Yeah,' I reply smiling at her. 'Solitaire is so important to the business isn't it?' Before she can reply I say, 'Never mind, Annette, they don't have to be here. I have a little present I want to give Sidney before I go on my leave. I'm sure he'll appreciate it. You just sit there and do your office clerky things and I'll be gone in no time.'

I stride purposefully towards McGuigan's office as Annette shouts over at me, 'What are you doing? You can't just go into his office.'

'I think you'll find that I can,' I reply and march straight in. I close the door behind me and see there is a lock on the inside which I use to prevent Annette from coming in after me.

I am only in the office for a matter of a minute, doing what I feel is necessary, which is made a little more difficult with Annette banging on the bloody door and shouting that she's going to ring him and tell him what I'm doing. Like she can see through doors! She is only a minor irritation and I can basically ignore her until I'm done.

I unlock the door and march past her. I can't understand what she is saying but she is clearly upset at me. I don't rightly care though. What can she say to me that I have any interest in anyway.

I get back into the lift and press for the ground floor and a minute later I'm walking back to my car. As I leave the car park I see McGuigan's red Lexus coming in, himself at the wheel. Seated next to him is Felicity Henderson and in the back is fat Jerry and my own line manager, Anthony Speakman (I actually feel sorry for Anthony because he is generally one of the good guys). They all look at me as I drive away, but I ignore them. I have a very real feeling that this will be the last time we will see each other. Especially after what I've just done in McGuigan's office.

I have already made a decision and it's based on something that both John and Felicity have suggested, believe it or not. I have decided that I am not going to go to my mother's tonight for sanctuary. Instead I am going to go on a little trip. I haven't got my passport and I'm not returning to the house for it, but I have got my wallet and my credit card so I can pretty much go anywhere I like within the country.

I head for the train station and dump my car on the station car park. I go into the concourse to the ticket booth and buy a one-way ticket to our nation's capital, London. Half an hour later, with my MacBook under my arm, I board a train heading for Euston station. Finding a window seat, I take out my phone from my trouser pocket and look at it. I have had it on silent all day and was not aware of all the messages. There are fourteen missed calls and slightly more texts. I can see that they are mainly from work and Jenny, mixed in with others that I do not know. Without reading any of them, I delete the lot and before I know it, I have fallen fast asleep as the train hurtles along at two hundred miles an hour straight towards London and most importantly, straight towards Agnes Carter.

CHAPTER A6
More Group Therapy

Another bloody group session.

As though these bloody things actually do anyone any good. We are all different, that's one thing I've learned here, if nothing else. We are all different with different issues, outlooks, thoughts and problems. We all have different ways of dealing with these and banging us all together, all us nutcases in one room, to openly talk about our very private lives, is counter-productive. Particularly in my case.

I find it increasingly hard to get involved to the level that Spectacles and Mister Andrews want me to. They say that these things will do me good but as I look around the room, at dwarfy Charlie and scabby Eddie, for example, I fail to see how these two retards can help me in any way regarding the situation I find myself in. I suppose the only positive I can gain by being in their presence is that at least I'm not them. I'm not that bad. Maybe they're trying to show me that my life may be bad, it may be terrible, yes. But it's not *that* bad.

'Alex. Do you want to make a contribution to what Tommy has just said?' says Spectacles, who, I am happy to say, has had his hair cut very short and actually looks less bald because of it. I look at Tommy, an average looking bloke with short blond hair that sticks up at the front like Billy Whizz from the Beano. I wonder if he is a fast runner.

'Not particularly,' I say and continue to look ahead, my arms folded across my chest with my hands resting on opposite shoulders, my legs jutting out and my body sloping as far down on this bloody uncomfortable plastic chair as I possibly can. I am not in the mood for this and want my body language to show it.

'Maybe if you sit up straight you might feel more with it,' says Spectacles, as if reading my mind.

'I'm fine as I am,' I say childishly. But after a few minutes I concede that it's much more comfortable to sit up straight. My back is beginning to ache.

I can hear them all talking around me but I am not listening to what they are saying. I have no interest in this type of thing. I much prefer the one to ones I have been having with Mister Andrews but he has recommended I take part in these sessions as part of the "treatment" as he calls it. I am only here because I have to be, and for no other reason. Anyway, whenever I open my mouth I always seem to "offend" some sensitive soul so it's probably best for all concerned if I just sit here and mind my own business for a couple of hours.

But Spectacles won't let me!

'Come on now, Alex,' he attempts once more. 'You of all people must have an opinion on that!'

There is something about the tone of his voice that breaks me from my trance and I sit a little straighter in the chair. I am aware that scabby Eddie has been speaking but I have no idea what about. Noticing the change in my manner, Spectacles sees the advantage and pushes his point home.

'What do you say, Alex? What is your opinion?'

'My opinion on what? I don't know if you've noticed at all but I really haven't been listening.'

'I know that,' he replies, but he doesn't seem angry. 'We were talking about violence and whether you feel that it can solve problems or merely add to them. What do you think? Do you think that violence solves problems?'

'Yes I do,' I reply.

'You do?'

'Yes. I've just said so. There's nothing wrong with your hearing,' I'm sure I've used that line with him before but he ignores my insolence.

'Interesting. In my experience I find it does more harm than good. Can you tell me why you think that violence can be a positive way to solve a problem?'

I look at him and wonder to myself that if this guy is supposed to be clever, much more clever than I, then why is he talking such utter bollocks. I reply, 'Because virtually every country in the world has an army. I think that there are a few who don't but they must have their own reasons why not. We needed to use violence to stop Hitler amongst others. So yes, I believe that there is a place for violence in society. In fact we wouldn't be enjoying the freedoms (Okay, I see the irony of that choice of word) we do, had we not employed violence in the nineteen forties. So, you see, history actually backs my argument up.'

He looks at me thoughtfully. I don't know whether he is giving credence to my words or is just happy that I've decided to engage in the conversation.

'Okay,' he says finally. 'I see your point but that's different. We are talking about violence amongst individuals to solve matters of a less, how can I put it, of a less political or global importance.'

'It doesn't matter about the size of it,' I tell him. 'It's about what's important to each of us. Take Eddie over there. What's important to his life is important to his life. He may not care about what's happening in Syria or Iraq or any other shithole in the world because it doesn't affect him. Okay, all that stuff is important in the grand scheme of things, but not in Eddie's scheme of things, or mine, for that matter. What I'm trying to say is that what's important to us, is important to us, no matter how big or small it is on the global scale. So if violence can work for the prime minister, or the president of America or whoever else, to solve their particular problems, then why can we not work the same methods at our own personal level? Believe you me, if I was six foot four and built like a brick shithouse then I can guarantee you that I wouldn't have taken half the crap I've taken in my life.'

'A very complete argument,' says Spectacles after some thought and begins to rattle his pen between his teeth. He turns to the rest of the group. 'Does anyone want to add to, or speak about what Alex has just said?'

They all either look at each other or look to their feet. I'm a bit annoyed that Spectacles hasn't answered my question but has used his lack of an answer to include others and sidetrack the issue. A while ago I would have kicked off, but today I just slouch back down and stick out my feet once again. If he doesn't want to play then that's up to him.

The conversation moves away to other things and once again I find that my mind is drifting off, my lack of interest total. Spectacles now seems content to leave me be and for the next half hour I sit in the silence that I had been enjoying until he rudely interrupted me.

Eventually the session finishes and we all get up to go back to our rooms or to the library or the games room, or wherever takes our fancy. My own personal preference is my room where I can watch television in peace, away from these other people who mean nothing to me.

As I go to leave, Spectacles calls me over and like the obedient child they want me to be, I walk over and look at him expectantly.

'Alex,' he says, looking at his clipboard. 'I believe Doctor Andrews wants to see you straight after this session. Can you go directly to his office, please.'

I shrug my shoulders indifferently and leave the room.

As I stroll down the corridor towards his office I wonder what it is that he wants to see me about. I half hope that he has a date for my release but a part of me is scared to leave this place. I've grown used to it, accustomed to it almost. Although I hate the place, it feels a lot safer in here than it does out in the big wide world and I suddenly fear that I'm becoming institutionalised. I don't know what I'm more scared of, being told I am being set free or being told I have to stay here indefinitely.

I knock on his door and enter when he shouts for me to do so and he looks up at me from behind his desk. He is on the telephone and from what I can gather he is talking about me. It's probably Spectacles giving him an update on how I have just behaved in the group therapy session. Standing to the side of his desk is a man I recognise from some weeks ago. He is the solicitor my mother and father acquired for me. Mister Thomas, I think he's called. He is a middle aged man with silver-grey hair and I don't quite know what to make of him. He was very quick agreeing to have me incarcerated into this place for an assessment. That was months ago and I'm still stuck here so I'm instantly wary of him.

Eventually Mister Andrews says goodbye to whomever he is talking to and hangs up. He sits back in his chair and indicates for me to sit down in the usual place.

'Alex, Alex, Alex,' he says, exhaling loudly. 'Alex Sumner. What am I to do with you?'

'You could always let me go home, Doc,' I say. 'Let's face it, I shouldn't be here really now should I?'

I look to Mister Thomas but he doesn't say anything.

'It's either here or a prison cell, I'm afraid,' he says. 'And believe me, right here is the place where you have needed to be.'

'What do you want me for?' I say sighing. I can't be doing with this kind of talk. I just wish he would get straight to the point. 'Why is Mister Thomas here? What's happened?'

'The authorities have contacted me about your situation,' says Thomas in his strange accent. I can't make out if it's Geordie or Welsh. 'Apparently your wife and Mr Michaelson want to drop all the charges against you.'

'What?' I say, 'All of them?'

'Yes, the lot. All of them. The assault charges and the criminal damage charges. However, I've to tell you that it doesn't come without certain sacrifices on your part.'

'Which are?' I ask.

'That you forfeit all rights to your house. Basically you sign everything over to her.'

The cheeky bitch!

'Can I be frank, Mister Thomas?' I ask, as though I'm going to be anything but.

'Go on,' he says.

'Why are they doing this now? What has changed in the last few weeks for them to suddenly want all this dropped?'

Mister Thomas sits down on the edge of the desk. 'I'm not too sure,' he says. 'I'm also to tell you that Jennifer wants a divorce and she is sorting out the paperwork as we speak. It appears that she wants you out of her life completely. Maybe that's why she's dropping the charges.'

I am not happy. It's clear to me the reasons for this. The cow wants to marry the wanker and they want me out of the picture altogether. Should I give them the satisfaction? I don't think so. I will make it as difficult for them as I possibly can. There is no way I'm giving her the house so she can move that tosser in. No way. It's my bloody house. It was my money, mine, that we put down for the deposit and I've been paying the mortgage for years. I'm not giving all that up so lover boy can simply move in and sleep in the bed I've paid for, sit on the couch I've paid for and sleep with the woman I've paid for.

Thomas can see that I'm not happy. In a very bad attempt to alleviate the situation before I completely blow my stack he says, 'Maybe it's for the best Alex. Maybe it'll be a clean slate for the both of you and you can move on with your life.'

'You what!' I yell and he momentarily moves his body back as he sits there. 'You are supposed to be on my side. That's what my mum and dad are paying you to be, you fucking idiot....For the best? The best for who? Best for them and probably best for you too because then you don't have to do much for the money you're being paid. Jesus Christ, man! You tell me to get a grip and it's you who needs to get a bloody grip.'

'Alex,' interrupts Mister Andrews. 'Try to control yourself.'

'Listen,' I say to Thomas ignoring him, 'You can go back to the bitch and you can tell her from me that she can have the house over my dead body. You got that? There is no way I'm giving them my share in the house. You can tell them that if they want it then they can buy me out and pay me for all the furniture and stuff that's still in there. But there is no way on this earth that they are getting it for free. Fuck off. No way.'

I stand.

'Where are you going?' asks Mister Andrews. 'Please sit down. You need to control yourself.'

'Control myself? I have every right to be bloody angry, Mister Andrews. Every right. So if I want to shout and swear at this fucking useless bastard then I bloody well will. It doesn't mean that I'm crazy.'

'Okay, Alex,' says Mister Thomas, holding up his hands like an Italian soldier. 'If that's how you feel then I will relay that back to her and her representatives. I am here to look out for you, honestly. I was just thinking that complying with this would look good to the courts and might help your situation here a little.'

'Yeah, it might help a little,' I reluctantly concede. 'But let's face it, my being here is not just down to what happened with my bitch of a wife and my so called mate, is it?'

He does not answer.

'Right,' I say now feeling calmer.

I turn to Mister Andrews. 'Is that all? Can I go now?'

He looks to Mister Thomas who nods at him. 'Yes Alex, you can go. But I would like to see you again first thing tomorrow morning. We have other things that we need to discuss.'

I do not say goodbye or go to shake Mister Thomas's hand or any of that old bollocks. The bloke has got on my nerves, coming in here and asking me to give my house away. He doesn't deserve to shake my hand. And so I walk to the door, open it and leave the room, careful not to slam it shut behind me. I stand outside for a moment or two and can hear the two of them beginning a new conversation and I wonder just how many of these conversations have been taking place about me, behind my back over the last few weeks. I never thought that I would ever be such a hot topic of conversation for so many people.

The sad thing about it is that none of what they are saying about me will be good and as I walk along the now too familiar whitewashed corridors back to the sanctuary and peace of my room, I don't know whether to laugh about that fact or feel sad.

For some strange reason I do both.

CHAPTER B6
Caught Short In Euston

Trains.

I bloody hate trains.

I hate the smell of them, the noise they make, the way they are nearly always late, the rudeness of some of the people who work on them. But most of all I hate the passengers they carry.

Jesus! I am in a bad mood.

But then who can blame me? I watch the trees and fields, villages, towns and houses as they fly past my window as the train speeds ever southward towards the big city. I have time to reflect on the events that have changed my life so dramatically.

So far, in the last twenty four hours, I've been told that my job is likely to be made redundant and then had it confirmed. I've been punched in the face by the man who is likely to take my job to which he has not been reprimanded and probably never will be. I have had my novel rejected by the one agent I thought would love it and I have lost my wife to a man I thought was my friend. Can anyone blame me for being in a bad mood or for reacting the way that I have? Well, can they? If anything, I think I've been pretty reasonable about the whole thing.

I realise I've been drifting off to sleep and wipe the dribble from my mouth that has leaked out while I've been sitting there. I look around the carriage at the few people who are travelling with me. All of them oblivious to what has happened to me. All of them not giving a shit about what has happened to me, come to that. But then, maybe they too have their own problems and, to be frank, I don't give a shit about whatever their problems are either.

An old man sleeps with his head resting against the window and is occasionally jolted awake as the train jerks, his head coming away and then hitting the glass sharply, only for him to settle back in the same position until it happens again and he repeats the whole process. A young woman sits at the table across from me, a young baby asleep in her arms and she looks lazily out of the window, glad of the respite that the sleeping infant now allows. There are more people further along the carriage. I can just see the tops of their heads. They are all being quiet and minding their own business, which suits me down to the ground.

My mind wonders back to many years ago and a familiar journey. I was carrying a number of bags and struggling on the platform with them when a kindly young man with a scraggly beard and a home made tattoo on his forehead stepped forward to assist me with my luggage. After helping me to store it safely, he decided to sit next to me and tell me about how he had just been let out of prison that very morning and was travelling home to his parents house in Spalding. He introduced himself as 'H'. Just 'H'. I didn't feel it was right, for some reason, to ask him what 'H' actually stood for, but after talking to him for a few minutes I presumed it was "Herbert" because that's exactly what he was. A right bloody Herbert! I should have taken it as a warning. But due to his kindness in helping me when I was struggling with my bags, and the fact that he had been incarcerated at her majesty's pleasure, for GBH apparently, I thought it prudent to humour him. However, after about half an hour of listening to him babbling on about how none of his problems were of his own making, I pretended to fall asleep so as to avoid hearing his shit.

I wonder now if I am so different to scraggly bearded 'H'. Am I responsible for my own problems and just looking to shift the blame away from myself and onto someone else? As I sit here on the train I decide to make a list, in my head, of the things that have gone wrong and to what degree I am responsible. Well it passes the time if nothing else.

Okay, number one. My job loss. Is this my fault? Why would they look at letting me go in favour of a red-nosed, useless, beer swigging tosspot? I know the answer to that question straight away and the answer is no, I am in no way responsible for any of that. The people making the decisions are halfwits and buffoons who don't know their arses from their elbows. The reason I am being let go and Jerry fat-twat has been given, for all intents and purposes, my job, is that he's an arse-licker and I'm not. He's quite prepared to stab people in the back to get on and I'm not. He will bow and say "Yes sir, three bags full sir," whereas I'm more likely to tell them how it is. It's this frankness of speech and not suffering fools that has got me on the wrong side of these idiots and, to be honest, as I sit here thinking about it, I'm glad to be leaving. They say (whoever "they" are) that cream rises to the top. What a load of old bollocks. In my experience back-stabbers and arse-kissers rise to the top and if you can do both, then you've got it made. The only regret I have as I sit here pondering it all, is that I will now be sacked and not be able to claim whatever pittance they would have been offering in a severance package. But then... so what. Bollocks to them all.

Moving to number two. Losing my wife to my one time friend. Was that down to me in any way? Can I be held in any way responsible for that? Have I neglected her at all? Well... I have let her pretty much do whatever she wanted. I was never the jealous type, (until now that is), and allowed her to go out with her friends and go to aerobics and all that other shite she was into. It looks now that the "other stuff" she was into was banging my mate when my back was turned. Okay, I can acknowledge that I did become a little obsessive with writing the book, but it was supposed to be for the benefit of us both. I could only do it once I was home from work and she was content to let me get on with it and for her to do her own thing. Even when we were together, when I wasn't writing or she wasn't at bloody Boxercise or whatever the latest trendy exercise fad was, she would just sit there in her scruffs watching shite TV. The novel was supposed to lead to fame and fortune and plenty of money where we both could give up our jobs and do as we pleased. So in conclusion on this particular issue, do I feel in any way to blame for any of this? Categorically no!

This kind of leads on to number three and the one that is hurting me the most, oddly enough. The novel itself. It has taken me over a year to write. I have meticulously researched it, planned it perfectly and written it very, very well. The characters are superbly constructed, the plot is totally believable leading to a denouement no-one will expect. It is a whole lot better than most of the trash you see in Waterstones or Tesco or wherever it is that people buy their books these days.

Okay, I know I am biased but it truly is a fantastic read and the email this morning from Agnes Carter, telling me in so few words that it's not for her was like a dagger deep into my heart. To use Jerry's turn of phrase, "like literally." She is supposed to be a top literary agent, one of London's best, but for her to treat my work with such utter contempt makes me now doubt that. But I will give her the benefit of the doubt. There may be mitigating circumstances surrounding the decision and I am prepared to give her another chance to redeem herself and take another look at it.

So my final conclusion, as I sit here watching passengers get on and off the train at Milton Keynes, is that, no, none of this stuff is in any way my fault whatsoever. I totally refuse to accept it.

The train eventually pulls into Euston Station and I grab my laptop and step onto the very crowded platform. Immediately I head for the concourse and as I enter it, I see that it is filled with masses of people all bustling about. Some are standing in other people's paths, looking up to the huge board above the entrances to the platforms, seeking out the one their train is to set off from. Others sit on the floor, their backs against the advertising hoardings, and others use their rucksacks and suitcases as temporary seating. I can see that all the eating establishments are doing a roaring trade, despite the ridiculous prices they are charging for their wares and on seeing them I realise that I haven't eaten in some considerable time and am suddenly very hungry.

I decide to grab a baguette from one of the vendors and choose a ham and cheese for simplicity. I ask for a bottle of water to wash it down and hand over the required amount of money. It's beyond me how they can charge so much for such a little bit of food and I'm about to have a go at the shop assistant but stop myself. It's not their fault, they're only trying to earn a living and they don't set the prices. Not their fault. Calm down Alex. Leave them alone.

I check my money and see that I have exactly twenty one pounds left. A twenty pound note and a one pound coin. I make a mental note that I must stop off at an ATM and replenish my wallet when I next pass one.

Finding a table in the communal eating area, I sit down. The table has the remains of the previous occupants meal still upon it, sheer laziness preventing them from clearing up after themselves. Spilt coffee stains the tabletop, forming elaborate shapes where some of it has dried and empty polystyrene cartons with half eaten burgers and cold french fries fill the space. I push the litter to one side and eat my rather tasteless and overpriced excuse for a meal and try to ignore the noise of the place. As well as hating trains, I hate train stations. I hate everything about the rail industry. All of it.

I finish the food and drink the bottled water. It's then that I realise that I need to go to the toilet and after I have placed my waste into a bin (unlike the dirty, lazy sods who occupied the table before me), I follow the directions to the left where I can see other people with full bladders walking through turnstiles to relieve themselves.

I approach the turnstile and then realise that I will actually have to pay for the privilege of using the station toilet. And it won't be a penny I'll be spending either, they want thirty pence. I check my change and realise that I only have the twenty pound note and the single pound coin. I stand there for a second or two, blocking one of the turnstiles as I look at the money in my hand. I can sense people behind me immediately getting impatient. Maybe I'm breaking some kind of London train station etiquette by not moving as fast as I possibly can and so I look over my shoulder and see a middle aged man looking at me as though I'm the most stupid person he has ever laid eyes on. He instantly pisses me off.

Before I can stop myself, not that I actually want to stop myself, I look directly into his eyes and almost shout, 'What the fuck are you looking at? Use one of the others if I'm not quick enough for you.'

He steps back in shock, looking at me with an expression of what I can only describe as horror and fright upon his face and quickly moves to another turnstile, pays his money and then swiftly moves into the toilets, all the time looking back over his shoulder at the headcase who has just verbally assaulted him. The knob. I shrug to myself. Whatever.

I step away from the turnstile and ponder my dilemma. I need to go to the loo, there's no doubt about it, but I'm also in no doubt that I'm not putting a pound into the turnstile to be able to do it. There's no way I'm paying a quid to have a pee!

I look around and see a WH Smiths. I walk over to the shop, thinking that I will buy a bar of chocolate and get some change for the machine, even though it pains me that I will have to pay thirty pence just to relieve myself. Absolutely ridiculous. It irritates me as much as having to pay parking on NHS car parks. "Rip-off Britain" definitely sums it all up. At least if I have to get change this way I will have a bar of chocolate to enjoy afterwards.

I walk to the confectionary stand and look at the offerings. There is too much choice. What to pick? As I stand there, my discomfort getting greater (I really need to go now), I see that the cheapest bar of chocolate is priced at a ridiculous, extortionate seventy three pence. Maths tells me that would leave me with twenty seven pence, three pence short of the required thirty I need for the mechanical device to let me into the toilets to relieve myself. Common sense should tell me that as I am so desperate for the toilet I should just bite the bullet, accept the hit, put the quid in and put it down to experience. But then common sense has kind of left me today, for if it hadn't, I would never have gone back to work and paid McGuigan's office a visit and left him the present I left him.

I follow the masses out of the station and turn to the left where I can see steps leading down to a main road and a pub opposite, The Royal George. At the top of these steps sits a tramp, a plastic cup in front of him next to a piece of cardboard, where he has written the words "HunGry and HomElEss".

I have an idea and, ignoring the bad grammar, I approach him and hold out the pound coin. I'd sooner this guy have the excess seventy pence than British Rail, or whatever they are calling themselves these days.

He looks up at me with tired eyes. His hair is long, his face dirty and bearded. I can't tell how old he is but there is not a grey hair on his head and so I presume he is quite young.

He does not say anything or even raise his hand to take the money, he merely nods to the plastic cup and then puts his head back down. My first instinct is to kick the ignorant, ungrateful bastard in the bollocks as he sits there, but I don't do that. I need him.

'Here, mate,' I say and he looks up at me again curiously. 'I want change.'

He bursts into laughter. 'Change? What do you mean?'

'I want change,' I repeat. 'If I give you this quid I want you to give me thirty pence back.'

'What do you think this is?,' he replies. 'A fucking bank? You give me the pound if you want to. But if you do, you're giving me a pound.'

I have to be honest, I'm pretty much taken aback by this guy's attitude.

'I'm giving you seventy pence,' I tell him. 'Why are you being ungrateful?'

'I'm not,' he replies. 'But I sit here all day with people either ignoring me or taking the piss. Let's face it, mate, if you didn't need change for something then you would have walked past me like ninety nine point nine percent of all the other people, wouldn't you? So, desperate as I am and no matter how shitty my life is, I still have my self-respect if not my dignity. So, either give me the quid or keep walking.'

'Come on, man,' I plead, stepping from foot to foot. 'I need it for the loo. I'm dancing here!'

'Well dance away, my friend, dance away.'

For some strange reason Bryan Ferry comes into my head.

I've had enough of this shit. Can my day get any worse? After all that's happened to me, I'm now being rebuked by a bloody tramp. A bloody dirty, scruffy, foul-mouthed loser, living on the bloody streets thinks that he is superior to me.

Maybe he is, I think. Maybe he is.

With nothing more to say to the guy, I put the pound coin back into my pocket and as he slumps his head forward once more, shutting his eyes in the process, I place a well aimed kick at his plastic cup, knocking it flying through the air, spilling its contents down the steps in the direction of the street below. Before he can react I turn and head back into the station, his shouts of abuse following me as I run. People, normal people, who have witnessed what I have done, look at me with horror and revulsion, but I don't care. I really don't give a shit right now.

I head back to the toilet area passing those coming out and overtaking some of those heading in the same direction. As I pass the shops and eateries I see the irony of what is happening here. Inside this concourse there are huge businesses and corporations that are trying to squeeze every penny out of me, while outside there is a homeless guy who won't accept my donation because it hasn't been given with a good heart. I would laugh out loud but I am trying so hard to stop myself from pissing my pants.

Holding it in is starting to hurt now. I'm in a desperate situation. I quickly pass the attendant, a man of around sixty years old and vault over the turnstile, nearly dropping my laptop as I do so.

'Hey, you,' I hear the attendant shout behind me. 'You can't do that. You haven't paid.'

I do not look back but place my laptop on a sink to the side and, facing a urinal, I unzip my flies.

The relief is immense. I instantly feel a thousand times better and it is probably the first time all day where I have felt relaxed and contented. Standing there, pissing into a porcelain urinal in Euston Station.

I become aware of the attendant standing to my side.

'Hey, you,' he says again and I turn my head to look at him. 'You haven't paid. You can't not pay! You're out of order. You have to pay like everybody else.'

'I had no change,' I reply. 'And it's too much to pay anyway. You're bloody robbing us.'

'You're very strange,' he replies. 'No-one else ever does this.'

'I'm strange?' I say raising my eyebrows. 'I'm strange? I'm not the one who's just followed a stranger into the toilets to watch him having a piss, you bloody weirdo!'

I can see the anger rising in his reddening face. 'I'll call the police. I'll call the police if you don't give me what you owe me.'

I look at him again and am shocked to see that he is actually holding out his hand. Others in the toilets pass us sideways glances, not wanting to get involved, the more hygienic ones hurriedly washing their hands, hoping to get out of the way in case the situation develops and they may have to bear witness. They don't want their journeys held up by having to give statements or anything daft like that.

I look down at his hand. 'I'm a bit pre-occupied at the minute,' I say. 'My hands are somewhat busy.'

'Well you're not leaving here until you give me what I want,' is his quite inappropriate reply.

I've had enough of this irritating little jobs-worth and turn to him. What I do next is done on impulse. Its a spontaneous thing, done without any thought process whatsoever. It merely happens and I don't seem to have any control over it. And what's more, what's most disturbing, is that I don't regret it.

Looking at his still open hand I turn and spray my urine at him, hitting his outstretched palm and fingers. He jumps back immediately and shouts at me, 'You dirty bastard. What do you think you're doing? It's disgusting.'

I have now finished and zip myself up. As I go to the sink to wash my hands and collect my laptop, the attendant is still shouting, telling me I am the most disgusting person he has ever met and that he is going to call the police.

Before I leave him, rinsing his hand under the tap, I say to him calmly. 'Call the police if you want, but believe you me, you bloody well deserved that.'

I leave quickly. I do not run but I walk with a purpose, which is pretty much the same way most people are walking in this place and I can understand why. They need to get out of the train station, away from all this bullshit.

I've been in London for only a matter of minutes and the place is already pissing me off. And I haven't even left the train station yet!

I exit the station and glance to my left, where I see that the ungrateful homeless guy has now moved on to another patch and is no longer to be seen. I sigh with relief because I do not want another altercation with him. I can do without it.

I head towards Upper Woburn Place and cross with the crowds at the traffic lights. I head south, in the direction of Russell Square and as I get to the Royal National Hotel I go inside. There are two receptions, one to the left and one to the right, separated by a large courtyard. I head to the right, past a bar where I can see many people enjoying an early evening drink and approach the reception desk.

A girl, no older than twenty years old, smiles at me and says, with a heavy Eastern European accent, 'Hello sir, can I help you?'

'Yes,' I reply. 'I would like a room for a couple of nights please.' I take out my wallet and search for my credit card. Finding it I place it on the desk in front of her.

'Do you have a reservation?'

'No.'

'That is no problem,' she replies, still smiling. Thank God for a friendly face, even if she is getting paid to smile at me.

I wait until she eventually finds a room. She takes the card from the counter and, by now, I really don't care what it costs. I just need to shower and then get my head down. I want this day to end, for it to be over, for it to be placed in a box, consigned to history with the label "Worst Day Of My Life" attached to the side.

She holds out a card machine and I input the PIN code without even looking at the cost. She hands me the keys, gives me some instructions on how to find the room and after nearly fifteen minutes of searching for it (this hotel is bloody huge) I eventually find it.

I take out my phone and see that I have more messages and more missed calls. The battery has only twenty two percent charge left on it and so I turn it off. Tomorrow I will have to find a shop and buy a charger for it. I will also need to buy some toiletries and a toothbrush and maybe a change of clothes, because I really have no idea how long I'm going to be away for. My head is now banging and the pain from my nose is getting worse. It's really bloody sore.

I shower and then, with the towel wrapped around me, I lie on the bed.

Tomorrow will be another day, I think, and no matter how bad it will be, it in no way can be any worse than the one I have just gone through. Tomorrow will be much better. Tomorrow will be a happy day, I can tell. I have a sense of optimism about the coming day, because tomorrow, I will finally get to meet Agnes Carter and after I speak to her, I know my life will change for the good. It has to. Surely it has to.

With this thought in my head I slowly drift off to sleep.

I dream of a party. It's a book launch and my book is everywhere, people are coming to me and congratulating me and I am signing copies for everyone. They are all there. Jenny is there, holding hands with the tramp from Euston Station. McGuigan is in the corner sipping champagne with Jerry red-nose. Annette and Felicity are dancing in the corner with the toilet attendant and John Michaelson is at the far side of the room frantically brushing his teeth with a toilet brush and a bottle of bleach.

It's all mixed up and messed around and when I awake the next morning I wonder if the dream was a damn sight less complicated than the reality of my life.

CHAPTER A7
An Assessment

'Can you tell me why you defecated in your boss's desk drawer?'

I laugh. 'I don't care what anyone says, its funny. My mind wasn't in the right place, I appreciate that now. I was going away and wanted to give him a present that fit in with what I thought of him. He'd been giving me shit for ages and I thought it only fair that I gave him some back.'

'Yes,' says Mister Andrews. 'In a TV comedy it may be quite amusing, I understand that. But this is your life we are talking about, Alex, not some sitcom or Jim Carey film. You do realise that it's not what rational people do? It's not what people do, even though they may think about doing it.'

'He deserved it,' I reply, 'Okay, it was a bit extreme, I'll grant you that, and maybe if my head was not so mashed up I wouldn't have done it. I'd just caught my wife, the woman I loved, with a guy I thought was my friend. I flipped out. Who can blame me?'

'Okay,' says Mister Andrews looking at me thoughtfully. He looks down again to the sheet of paper he has in front of him and I have the distinct feeling he is reading from a list. A list of all my misdemeanours. 'The attendant at Euston Station. You relieved yourself on him. Again, this is not something a sane person would do.'

'He deserved it too. He was a prick.'

'I understand, to a certain degree mind, that you wanted to punish your boss. I understand that your mind was not at the level it should be at, considering what had happened to you that day. But the toilet attendant was a stranger. He had done nothing to you. He meant nothing to you.'

'True,' I respond.

What is he getting at here?

'You see, it's difficult for me,' says Mister Andrews, changing the course of the conversation slightly. 'I have to assess you. I have to let the courts know whether I think this was a breakdown due to your loss of job, wife's adultery and the rest... something that is unlikely to happen again. Whether this is a one off and the violent behaviour you have exhibited is a thing of the past and unlikely to be repeated. Unless I am convinced that this is the case, I can't recommend you for release. Even if you are released, you still could face criminal charges.'

'If I was off my rocker at the time then doesn't that help my defence?'

He looks at me.

'Maybe,' he replies, 'but whether you were "off your rocker" as you so eloquently put it, or not, it could still mean time spent in prison. You have to be aware of that.'

'I don't remember being violent to anyone.'

'That's what worries me.'

Shit. The man has a point.

I have no recollection of hitting anyone, trying to hit anyone, or doing any of the things that they say I did. I do remember throwing the tray at the nurses a couple of weeks ago and it did quite scare me that I was capable of doing that. I also remember rubbing the toilet brush in Michaelson's face. But then, any other husband would do something similar if they had just caught their wife with them. Wouldn't they?

What I don't remember is attacking Jenny. I'm not even convinced it actually happened. All I remember is leaving the house and pissing in that knobhead's car. I don't remember doing to her what they say I did. And if I did, then who's to say it wasn't an accident?

'You did a lot of things that would be considered, how can I put this... abnormal, during that period. You have continued, if I may talk frankly, to be a pain in the arse at the group therapy sessions, upsetting other residents... '

'Inmates, Doc,' I reply. 'This is hardly a hotel now, is it?'

'We prefer to use the term "residents,"' he replies and I can tell he is slightly annoyed. Which amuses me.

'Inmates,' I repeat insolently.

'This is the type of thing I'm talking about,' he says, throwing his arms up. 'Exactly this. You can't help yourself can you? You really aren't helping yourself.'

'Oh, Doc,' I sigh. 'That's the trouble with the world today. No sense of humour. You should be pleased with me, not the opposite. After all that's happened to me, I can still make jokes and laugh at things. I should be applauded for it.'

'Joking is fine,' he says, 'But it has to be done in the right way. It always seems to be at someone else's expense with you.'

'No, Mister Andrews,' I say. 'It's just that I learned to stop suffering fools. It's as simple as that.'

He doesn't reply to this but decides to change tack.

'Are you still having problems in the morning… when you wake up?'

'Meaning… ?'

'You had an issue with waking up in floods of tears. Is it still happening?'

'Occasionally,' I lie. It's still every day.

'What are your dreams about?'

'I forget them as soon as I wake up. I just know that I've dreamed but I have no idea what about.' (The truth).

'Hmmm,' he says thoughtfully and seems to be contemplating saying something else but stops himself. Then he says, 'They want a report by the end of next week and I have to be honest, Alex, I am struggling a little bit with it. I need you to show some effort before then otherwise I can't recommend you leaving here. I need something positive from you.'

It is an hour later and I am lying on my bed looking up at the white ceiling, with it's fan turning slowly in a clockwise direction, sending down a slight breeze onto my face that I find refreshing in the heat of the afternoon.

Maybe Mister Andrews has a point. Maybe I have been doing things that are not "normal" and are unacceptable. Maybe, if I want to get out of this place, I will have to conform to what they are saying. Go back to suffering those fools and just forget about it. Accept that there are people in this society, in this world, that will get on my nerves and I will just have to learn to ignore them. But it's so hard when they have a controlling influence on your life, like McGuigan and Henderson used to have. So very hard.

The stories of violent behaviour on my part are a serious concern for I don't remember most of it. It's as though my mind has blanked it out because it's so out of my character. I can't deny it happened because the evidence is there. I have even been shown some of the CCTV footage and it's clearly me. I just don't remember doing it. Just like I don't remember the few hours before my eventual arrest. None of it.

I have to accept that there is something clearly wrong with me. I have denied it long enough, I suppose, but unless I take some responsibility and listen to these people then I will never get out of this "One Flew Over The Cuckoo's Nest" bloody place. I can't restructure my life stuck in here. I need to be outside where I can sort things out. Find a job. Find new friends. Get back on track.

Eventually the spinning ceiling fan has a soporific effect on me and I find my eyes becoming heavy. A few minutes later I am sound asleep.

CHAPTER B7
Agnes Carter

I dress and go down to breakfast. However, when I get to the "dining room", as they call it, I realise that it is little more than a canteen with rows of tables set out like at school. After queueing for ten minutes with a horde of French and Japanese tourists, no doubt getting excited about forking out their hard earned cash on overpriced tickets to the London Eye or some other such so-called attraction, I give up and leave the hotel in search of a cafe where I will be able to have a less haphazard meal experience.

I find a small coffee shop further along the road, towards Russell Square, and order a coffee and a bacon sandwich, which I again pay over the odds for. However, by now I have reluctantly accepted that prices in the capital are somewhat higher than back home and so hand over the money without complaint. I even leave a small tip. God ,I'm feeling good today!

My phone buzzes in my pocket and I take it out. It's my mother ringing me again. I ignore it, turn off the thing and put it back in my pocket. I really don't want to speak to anyone from home right now. In fact, I don't want to think about home at all today. I need my focus to be on the task in hand and not reflecting on yesterday's events. I will go mad if I think about any of it.

I wander for an hour in the general direction of Soho, looking in shop windows and watching all the weirdos who inhabit this city, for there are many, go about their business. There are loads of tourists from all over the world, and many other people who rush around, jumping out in front of traffic, the drivers slamming on their brakes and shouting abuse out of open car windows. The sound of pneumatic drills add to the general noise and hubbub and I understand why it is that I live in the suburbs of a smaller city. The big city life is not one for me. No way. It'd do my head in!

Eventually I reach my destination, an office block down a short side road, and I go through large double doors into a wide reception area. A middle aged woman sits behind a large desk, a row of three lifts to her right. A security guard stands watch on the opposite side. A board at the side of the desk indicates which companies occupy which floors and I stand a few feet away, looking at it intently. I can sense both of them looking at me curiously, no doubt my somewhat dishevelled appearance giving them a little concern. My two black eyes aren't helping either, I suppose.

'Can I help you, sir?' says the receptionist in quite a posh London accent.

'Erm, yes,' I respond. 'Can you tell me which floor I can find Carter, Mayhew and Bell, literary agents? I can't seem to find them on the board.'

'Do you have an appointment?' she asks, staring at my blackened eyes.

'No, but I'm sure it'll be fine. It's Agnes Carter who I need to see.'

'Without an appointment, there's nothing I can do. You will have to ring and make one.'

'Well I'm here now,' I say. 'I've come a long way to see her. Can't you just tell me which floor they are on and I'll be out of your way.'

'Like I've just told you,' she says pompously, 'You need an appointment.'

'I have ears,' I respond. 'And I understand English. I know what you bloody well said. I am merely asking you to ring up and see if she'll see me.'

I can see the security guard stepping forward slightly.

'I will ask you to refrain from speaking to Miss James like that,' he says.

I look at him and take a breath.

'I'm sorry,' I say. 'It's just that I've come a long way and need to see her. All I'm asking is for you to ring up and ask if she'll see me.'

'Without an appointment it's pointless,' says Miss James. 'You really need to leave.'

I look again at the board and this time am able to spot that Carter, Mayhew and Bell are on the sixth floor. I stand there, in front of them, not moving. The security guard seems unsure on what to do and as we contemplate this Mexican stand-off, one of the lift doors opens and a couple of men walk out. They pass us, oblivious and uninterested in what is taking place in the foyer, and exit out of the main doors and onto the Soho streets.

I watch them leave and as I turn my head back I see that both the security guard and Miss James are still staring at me. I turn to look towards the lift the two men have just exited, and before the security guard can stop me, I walk purposefully toward it.

'Hey. Come back. You can't go in there,' he shouts after me but I ignore him. As far as a security guard goes, this one is pretty crap. I press the button for the sixth floor and as the doors start to close I see him half-heartedly running to the doors. I manage to show him the middle finger of my right hand as the doors close and the lift starts to move up.

I watch the display as it moves up the floors and eventually it stops on the sixth floor and I step out. I did not realise how big a building it was until now. Again there is a reception area and corridors lead to the left and right. There are many different businesses occupying this floor and as I stand there, a much nicer receptionist, a young blonde who is very attractive, looks over at me.

'You look lost,' she says, smiling at me. 'Who is it you are looking for?'

I approach the desk.

'Hiya,' I say, smiling back at her. 'I'm looking for Agnes Carter of Carter, Mayhew and Bell. Can you tell me where I can find her?'

'Do you have an appointment?' she asks.

Bloody hell. Here we go again.

'Yes,' I lie. I've learned my lesson on that particular issue.

'Right,' she replies and stands up. Leaning over the desk she holds out her arm, pointing down the corridor to her left. 'If you follow the corridor through the double doors you will find her in the second office on the right.'

I follow where she is indicating and when I look back to her she is still leaning over the desk slightly and I am able to see down her top at what I can only describe as a perfect cleavage. I'm a bloke after all. Flesh and blood. She sees my gaze and sits back, her arm instinctively going across her chest. Her face reddens and I am aware that I am blushing too. It was just one of those things. Can't be helped.

I quickly say thank you and then walk through the double doors. I get to the room she has indicated and see the sign "Agnes Carter - Literary Agent" on the door. I take a breath and knock.

There is no answer and so after a few seconds I knock again. I wait a little longer and then put my ear to the door, listening for any sign of life from the other side.

Suddenly the door opens and I nearly fall into the room.

Agnes Carter. The Agnes Carter. She stands in front of me, a mobile phone clamped to her ear and deep in conversation. She waves me in and points to a seat in front of a very untidy desk, as though she's been expecting me.

I don't think I have ever seen such an untidy office in all my life. There are boxes and boxes dotted all around the room, which is not as big as you would expect for such a high flyer, and masses of papers cover her desk along with various items of stationery. A computer monitor and a keyboard half covered with paperwork sit in the middle of the desk and there are three mugs lined up to the right. One of them says "You don't have to be mad to work here..." which I find sums up the craziness of the state of the office.

I take a look at her. I wouldn't say that she is exactly like, or exactly unlike the picture on her website. More somewhere in the middle perhaps. I would probably say that she is "similar" to the website photograph if anything. She is quite short, a little on the chubby side and has quite small features. Her hair is dark and cut in a bobbed style, with a fringe that looks like it needs cutting as it keeps falling into her eyes, causing her to push it back from her face with her well manicured and bejewelled fingers.

Occasionally she looks at me as she talks and raises her eyebrows as though it's a conversation she can't be bothered with and now and again she raises her hand and does a chopping motion with her thumb and fingers, the universal sign for someone who is rabbiting on a bit too much. I smile indulgently.

Eventually she manages to get in a couple of 'goodbyes' and with a promise of continuing the conversation tomorrow, she finally hangs up and places the phone onto her madcap desk.

She intertwines her fingers and rests her elbows on the desk, ignoring the fact that she has knocked a pen to the floor in doing so.

'I can't get anything done these days,' she says. 'It's non-stop every day. All day. I don't get a minute's peace.'

'I know how you feel,' I reply because I can't think of anything else to say.

Now that I'm here, I really don't know what to say to her. There were a thousand things I was going to say. At first I was going to have a go at her, tell her what an idiot she is and what a big mistake she's made, but then I thought this might be counter-productive and so I've changed my plan and decided that I will ask her to reconsider and take another look at the manuscript.

For the first time since I entered the office she looks at me.

'What the bloody hell happened to you?' she asks. 'Your face!'

'Oh,' I reply. 'A little bit of a misunderstanding. Nothing to worry about.'

'Jesus, it looks sore,' she says. 'Are you all right?'

'Not particularly but I'll be fine,' I reply.

'What time did you get in?' she asks. 'I wasn't expecting you for another hour or so.'

It's at this point that I realise that I'm not the person who she thinks I am. Oh my God. How disappointed is she going to be!

I decide to play along for a while.

'I got in last night,' I say. 'Early evening.'

She looks aghast.

'Last night? My secretary told me you were only landing this morning. If I'd known you were getting an earlier flight then I would have taken you out last night. Why didn't you tell me?'

It's no use. There's no way that I'll be able to keep this up for very long so I decide to put her straight.

'Who do you think I am?' I ask.

Then it dawns on her and she raises her eyebrows. Well at least I think she does, I can't really tell because of the fringe.

'You're not Pieter Koekemoer?'

'No. Why would you think that? Do I sound South African? I presume he's South African with a name like that. Do I look like I've just got off a plane?'

I just can't help myself. Why am I like this?

She is clearly taken aback by what I have said.

'Who are you? Why have you come into my office pretending to be my new client?'

'I've done no such thing. I've never claimed to be your new client, Peter Coconut, or whatever his bloody name is.'

Truth be told, I am heartbroken. It's clear that she is as much a bloody imbecile as all those other idiots I've had to contend with over the past couple of days. All those morons from work and those dickheads I've come across in London. And this silly cow has emailed me to tell me that my work isn't up to the required standard. Has she seen her office, the stupid bitch?

However, she has connections and even though I want to sit here and tell her what I think of her, I stop myself. She could still hold the key to my future.

'Then who are you and what the hell are you doing in my office?'

'You told me to come in,' I say, and instantly realise I am being facetious and insolent. 'But I did come to see you, Miss Carter,' I add in a gentler tone.

'Who are you?'

'You sent me an email yesterday,' I explain. 'My name is Alex Sumner.'

I can see her wracking her brains, searching in her mind for some kind of recognition of my name.

'Alex… ' she says meditatively.

'Sumner,' I complete my name for her.

'No,' she says suddenly and sharply, shaking her head from side to side. 'I'm sorry. Too much info in this little head of mine. Can't seem to recall your name. What was it about?'

'You can't recall my name?' I ask, dumbfounded. 'You sent me the email less than twenty four hours ago.'

'A lot can happen in my life in twenty four hours.'

I stare at her but can't fault what she has just said. Ain't that the truth! I think 'same here', but I don't say it out loud.

'Remind me,' she orders.

'I sent you a submission recently,' I tell her, although she should already bloody well know this. 'It was for my novel. You sent me an email yesterday.'

Realisation dawns on her face. At first I think it's because she has finally recognised my name but then understand, almost a second later, that it's because it's quite the opposite. She does not remember my name at all. In fact, I wouldn't be surprised if this is the first time that she has ever heard of me, or even been aware of my actual existence.

'You have absolutely no idea who I am, do you?' I ask.

She holds up her hands.

'Forgive me, Mister Summers,' she says. 'Alec... can I call you Alec?'

'No you bloody well can't!' I reply. She frowns at me. 'My name is Alex,' I say. 'Alex with an X not Alec with a C. Alex! Bloody Alex! And my surname is Sumner, 'Ner, bloody 'Ner! Not Alec Summers!'

For the first time she looks genuinely afraid of me.

'I don't think I like your attitude, Mister Sumner,' she says. 'If you can just calm down and tell me exactly what it is you want from me.'

'You sent me an email yesterday rejecting my submission,' I tell her, although, like I say, she should already know this. 'You sent me exactly two lines... twenty five words... seventy nine characters... telling me my work wasn't up to scratch.'

'You counted them?'

'Yes, I counted them,' I answer. 'But it looks to me that you haven't even looked at my work. Do you know how long it took me to write that novel? To write it and edit it and re-write it and re-edit it? Many times until it was perfect. No? Well I'll tell you. It took me well over twelve months. Every night when I got in from work, for almost the past year and a half, I've taken myself upstairs and worked on it. It's now led to my wife buggering off with another bloke and me losing my job... and you haven't even looked at it.'

She holds up her hands in a kind of surrender.

'Okay, Mister Summers... Sumner. I can see you are upset and I'm sorry to hear about your wife and job, but that has little to do with me. I appreciate the effort you have put into your work and I'm sorry that Tania thinks it isn't suitable for my list.'

'Tania... ? Who the bloody hell is Tania?'

Yes, who the hell is Tania?!

'Tania is the intern here. She is on a year's work placement while she does her degree. She filters all the submissions and passes those she thinks have merit on to me.'

I can't believe what I'm hearing.

'So you have a young nineteen year old girl, with no experience whatsoever, telling you that my novel is shit? Is that about the size of it?'

'Well I wouldn't have put it quite like that. She is a very talented individual and her judgement is very good... '

'Hardly,' I interrupt. 'If she had good judgement I would be sitting opposite you now and you would be offering me representation. There's no doubt about it.'

'Do you know how many submissions we get each week, Mr Sumner?' I shake my head. 'Well I'll tell you. Every week we receive over two hundred submissions and, to be fair, the majority of them are fine. We do get a lot of rubbish, granted, but in the main they are quite good. But being quite good does not cut it in this business, believe me. A submission has to leap out at us, it has to jump out of the pile like a salmon in a river. It has to grab our attention in such a way that we are compelled to read more... that we'll just die if we don't get more. That we need to read it all. But, alas, this rarely happens. Very rarely. But when it does, that's when we give you a call. That's when we have you in this office and discuss a way forward.'

'If that's the case then I'm surprised you have an amateur going through them. They are bound to miss some good stuff.'

'Possibly,' she continues. 'But there are only so many hours in a day, so many days in a week and besides looking at all the new stuff, we have our established clients that we need to look after, not to mention life itself. I have three children, Mister Sumner. All at school. When I get home from work I don't spend all my spare time working. I actually like to watch television now and again, spend time with my family. You know, normal stuff. That's why we work the way we work.'

I sit back in my chair. I never knew that the life of a literary agent was so busy and I can understand her points. But to have a rank amateur sending me a stock email that my work is crap does not sit right with me.

'Can I ask you one favour?' I ask. 'Seeing I have come all this way to see you and the effort I have put into the novel?'

'Go on,' she says reluctantly.

'Could you please look at my submission personally? If you do then I will leave it and hassle you no more.'

She doesn't speak for a moment or two but looks into my desperate eyes. Eventually she sighs and leans back in her chair.

'To be honest,' she says. 'I should call security and have you thrown out of the building and I should then find your submission and shred it. But I won't do that. If you promise to leave me alone and never come back into this building unless invited, then I promise to take a look at your work.' I smile and am about to thank her but she holds up her hands. 'Just understand that this is not a promise of anything more than me taking a look. This is no offer of representation or anything like that. And to be honest, if Tania has seen fit not to pass it on then she will probably have had good reason.'

Now she let's me respond.

'Thank you, Miss Carter,' I say. 'That's all I ask. To be given a proper shot at it. Whatever your decision is, then I will accept it and move on.'

'Good,' she says. 'Now will you please leave my office. I have an important client due any minute and he has come a little further than you have to see me. Halfway round the world in fact.'

'The coconut fella?' I ask and for the first time since she realised I was not he, she smiles.

'Yes,' she replies. 'The coconut fella.'

And then she studies my face, and as if she has only just noticed she asks, 'What happened to your face?'

'Don't ask,' I reply. 'It's a long story and it's been a long couple of days.'

God it hurts!

'Okay,' she says, instantly uninterested. 'Now please go before I change my mind.'

I stand up and leave the office, closing the door quietly behind me, leaving her staring after me as I go. I am not sure if she will do as she has promised but I suppose I have to trust someone at some point and will have to take her word for it. As I walk past the reception desk to the lifts I see the pretty blonde girl on the telephone and glance over, hoping to get another look at her cleavage but she is deep in conversation. She looks up at me as I press the button and smiles at me slightly. I go to raise my hand in farewell but quickly put it down again in embarrassment. It doesn't feel right. As she talks on the telephone, she continues to look at me and when our eyes catch again she looks away.

The doors open and I enter the lift and as it descends to the ground floor I get the distinct feeling that the pretty girl on the sixth floor reception desk was talking to someone about me.

Am I going paranoid? I'm not too sure, but as I exit the lift into the ground floor reception area I suddenly feel extremely claustrophobic and have a massive urge to get out of the building and into what fresh air can be found on these smelly London streets.

I rush through the reception area to the double doors, ignoring the looks of the middle aged receptionist and the ineffective security guard, and when I eventually make it out onto the street, I find that I have to bend over double and take deep breaths. For some strange reason an old "Smiths" song enters my brain and I can hear Morrissey's voice pounding in my head, alongside the pneumatic drill that still hammers the street somewhere close by.

Eventually I can stand it no longer, and, finding a wheelie bin at the top of the alleyway to the side of the building, I lift the lid and vomit the contents of my breakfast into it.

CHAPTER A8
A Cup Of Coffee And A Chocolate Bar

I wake up and stare at the ceiling. The fan is still turning and what was a nice breeze earlier, keeping me cool and all that, has now turned into a the opposite and become a cold draught which is making me shiver, despite me being under the bed covers.

I get from under the sheets and sit on the edge of the bed. I lean over and turn off the fan and as it slows down to a stop, I am aware of the silence in the building. Looking over to the digital clock on the wall I see that it is half past one in the morning.

I am now wide awake and know that if I lie back down, I will probably be there for hours getting frustrated at not being able to get back to sleep, so I decide to get out of bed and find something to do.

I suddenly feel the need to eat. My appetite has not been good for a long long time and I have lost a bit of weight over the last few months, which hasn't been such a bad thing because I was a bit of a fat git before, if truth be told. I look in the drawer at the side of the bed and see that I have a few quid in loose change. There are a couple of vending machines just down the corridor, selling crisps, chocolate and hot drinks and I decide that I fancy a Mars bar.

I put on my white dressing gown and put the change into the pocket. I leave the room and can see the nurses station at the end of the corridor. The pretty one, whose name I have never got to know, is on duty tonight and she looks up as my door opens. I wave to her and point to the vending machine and she nods her head in acknowledgement.

I am unsure if she still sees me as a threat to her. Probably not. I have changed a bit since the early days of being in here. I am not the same person and hopefully, Mister Andrews and the Spectacles fella, Doctor Green, will soon acknowledge that.

I get to the machine and look at what is on offer. I have never used the thing before and nearly laugh out loud at the prices. The cheapest bar of chocolate is eighty pence.

The irony of the vending machine prices is not lost on me. My mind flashes back to a few months ago at Euston station and how I got so worked up over a bar being charged at seventy three pence, a whole seven pence cheaper than in here. Thank God the toilets in this nuthouse are free! Reluctantly I put in the money, press B5 and watch as the twirly thing on the B5 shelf spins around to release my Mars bar.

As I stand there chuckling to myself, no doubt looking like a complete head-the-ball, I hear a noise coming from one of the rooms to my right. It sounds like a child weeping.

At first I think of calling over to the nurse but my own curiosity gets the better of me and I approach the room to where the sound is coming from. Putting my ear to the door I listen carefully and hear it more clearly now. The occupant inside is crying. Crying like a baby.

I look at the card on the door and see Eddie Scraggs's name on it. Scabby Eddie. That smelly, dirty bastard.

I knock softly on the door and suddenly the sound stops. Not bothering to await permission, I open the door and step inside.

Eddie is sitting on the bed facing the door, a glass of water in his hand. He is dressed in the pyjamas the hospital staff have given him and his beard and hair look more dishevelled than ever. He has a bedside lamp switched on which casts light over the right hand side of his face, but leaves the left in slight darkness. The bulb must be of a very low wattage. I am grateful for this because the man is truly one ugly shit. I have a momentary feeling of jealousy as, for some reason, I'm not allowed a lamp. They probably think that I may use it as a weapon on the staff, which, to be honest, may have been the case a few short weeks ago. But not now.

He looks up at me as I close the door behind me with a look of what I can only describe as dread... or is it fear?

'What do you want?' he asks, between sobs. 'Why have you come in here? You shouldn't be in here.'

'Don't worry,' I reply. 'I couldn't sleep and heard you.'

'You shouldn't be in here,' he repeats, wiping his nose on his sleeve.

'Jesus, man!' I say, disgusted. 'That's minging. Use a bloody tissue or something.'

'Oh, piss off you,' he replies. 'Just leave me alone. You are horrible and no-one likes you. Just leave me alone.'

I look at him, sitting there all pathetic on the edge of his bed. For some strange reason, despite his bad attitude towards me, I feel a little sorry for him. I suppose we all have our own stories in here. We all have reasons for being locked up and kept away from society, whether for our own good or the good of others. Or both. Who is to say that my story is any worse than his? That my situation is more important than his? But then I don't know the man. I have never tried to get to know the man. Or anybody else in here for that matter. He has meant absolutely nothing to me. Nor I to him.

'I'll let that go,' I say, 'because you are clearly upset about something.'

He looks at me but says nothing.

I walk to the bed and sit on the edge next to him.

'Why are you crying, Eddie?'

'None of your business, Sumner,' he replies. 'Why would I tell you? All you ever do is take the piss out of people and feel sorry for yourself. We have absolutely nothing in common, me and you.'

I think about his words for a few moments. Part of me wants to elbow the ungrateful arsehole in the face, but another side of me, the side that is really me, wants to put an arm around him. Well maybe I won't do that. He fucking stinks.

Do I really feel sorry for myself? Well maybe I do. After all, up until very recently I had a good job, beautiful wife and thought I had a best seller on the cards. Now I am an inmate (they say I am a resident but we all know we are inmates) in this bloody place. Locked up with morons, retards and sociopaths. Why shouldn't I feel a little sorry for myself?

Is it really true about people not liking me? I used to worry about what people thought of me, but now I don't really care too much. But I always thought I was likeable. I always thought that I was a good egg and everyone wanted to be my mate. It looks like if I was once like that, I certainly am not anymore. I feel a certain amount of sadness at the thought.

'You know what, Eddie?' I say to him with a sigh. He looks at me, wiping the tears away from his eyes. This time on his other sleeve. I am about to say something about it but stop myself. 'You know what? We've had therapy sessions with the doctors here about our problems and I've never felt that I've really got anywhere. They can't understand how we function. They can't empathise with us, even if they think they can. They should just leave us be with each other and maybe we all might get somewhere. At least we all have an understanding of what it means to be in this state. To be totally lost without any hope. You know... actually in it. They can never feel how we feel.'

He looks at me as though I'm taking the piss again, but I can tell that he can't be sure.

I hold out the Mars bar to him.

'Here,' I say. 'Take it. Consider it a peace offering.'

He looks at me unsure.

'Go on,' I say, moving it closer to him. 'I've just bought it. That's why I'm out of my room. You can have it if you want. It cost me eighty pence. It wasn't cheap.'

He takes it from me and puts it on his bedside table next to the lamp.

We sit in silence for a few moments and eventually his sobs stop. He looks at me but I don't look back.

'What's your story, Alex?' he asks. 'Why are you in here. It's clear to the rest of us that you aren't stupid or anything. You seem a bit out of place. How did you end up in here?'

I turn to him.

'You know what, Eddie, I have absolutely no idea. None whatsoever. I had a bad time a few months ago and didn't deal with it very well. A lot of things went wrong for me and I let it build up, I suppose. And then I snapped. It didn't help that I was whacked in the head though. I'm sure that had something to do with it. Then I went doolally, to tell you the truth. Started behaving irrationally, with no thought for anyone, including myself, if I'm honest. No thought for my family, friends or anyone. I even became violent. I really don't want to go into it. It's all a bit embarrassing now, when I think about it.'

He doesn't say anything. What can he say?

Eventually I ask: 'And you? What's your story?'

'Same as you,' he replies, then quickly adds, 'without the violence, of course. I'm not a violent man. Some things happened to me and I started drinking. Drinking heavily. I used to have a good life… and a good job, up until a couple of years ago. I never used to be like this… or look like this. I lost someone I loved very much and I fell apart.'

He starts to cry again. I can see the memories of what he is telling me are hurting him deeply. I almost feel privileged that he is telling me this. Trusting me with this after all the shit I've been giving him.

I feel like leaving the room. I feel like walking out and leaving him to it but something inside me stops me. I want to revert to type and call him a retard and a smelly bastard and all the other things I have cruelly called him in the therapy sessions, but this time I don't. This time I don't have it in me.

'Who was it?' I ask. 'Who you lost.'

'My daughter,' he says quietly. 'She got a disease and died. She was only ten years old. I cry myself to sleep every night and cry in the mornings when I wake up. I started drinking and my wife left me. She couldn't cope with it all. I wasn't strong for her when I needed to be. I was a wreck.' He leans back and closes his eyes. 'I am a wreck.'

I get off the bed and take the change from my pocket.

'How much is coffee in this place?' I ask him.

'I'm sorry?' He is confused at my sudden change of conversation.

'The coffee in the vending machine. How much is it?'

'Oh I don't know. A quid I think. Not much more than that.'

'Do you want one?'

He looks at me again. Suspiciously.

'What is it you want, Sumner?' he asks.

'You know what, Eddie,' I reply. 'If I could answer that question I would be out of this place in no time.'

I leave the room and go to the coffee machine. The young pretty nurse approaches me.

'Alex, you need to be in your room. You can't go wandering the corridor at this time of night.'

Taking the second cup from the machine I look at her and reply: 'No you're wrong. My room is the one place I don't need to be right now.' I indicate the door to Eddie's room. 'Now if you would be so kind as to get the door for me, I would be very grateful.'

Not wanting to cause a scene, or unsure of my unpredictable nature, especially when I have two cups of hot coffee in my hands, she relents and opens the door.

'Okay,' she says, 'but I'll be back in half an hour and then I will have to insist you go back to your room.'

'It's a deal,' I say. 'You can close the door if you want.'

She sighs and shuts the door behind her.

'Now, Eddie,' I say handing him a coffee, 'Let's have a chat.'

#

I leave Eddie's room before the nurse returns and go back to my room.

I lie on the bed and stare at the white ceiling which looks grey in the darkness. I put my hands over my face and although I don't want to and try my hardest not to, I cry.

I cry like a baby, sobbing my heart out as though the world is about to end. And there is only one thought that goes through my head.

One thought only.

Just what the hell am I doing in here?

CHAPTER B8
Panic On The Streets Of London

I find a pub around the corner that has opened early and order a neat whiskey. I need to calm my nerves. I can't stop shaking. The barman looks at me suspiciously, is about to ask if I'm all right but thinks better of it and simply gets me my change without saying anything. I take it and put it in my pocket without checking it and find a table in the corner to sit down.

I hold out my hand in front of me and see that it is shaking, like an alcoholic in need of a drink, and my mind starts to run away with itself. I can't think straight. I can't seem to compute the smallest thing. I feel dizzy and am sure that if I'm not sitting down then I will probably fall flat on my face. I try to think back at what has just happened and there are blanks. I remember being in Agnes Cartwright's office but have no recollection of how I got there. Agnes Cartwright. Even her name doesn't sound right. Cartwright? Cart something. Carter. That's it Carter.

Christ, my head hurts!

What is happening to me?

My mind is all over the place again. Thoughts are jumping in and out of my brain in no apparent order and I can't seem to process them properly. They're all jumbled up.

I can sense the barman looking over at me curiously but when I meet his gaze he looks fuzzy and out of focus. He turns his head away awkwardly, embarrassed to have been caught staring at me. I shake my head from side to side in an attempt to re-boot myself.

I suddenly have a sane moment and wonder if pouring alcohol into my system is a good thing to do when I'm feeling like this. I stand up and approach the bar, leaving the whiskey unfinished on the table. I ask for a glass of mineral water and hand over more money. He puts it in front of me and I pour it down my throat hungrily and ask for another. I check my change and see that I have just enough for one more.

Slowly my senses start to come back to me and I'm able to think clearly once more. I'm shocked at this sudden panic attack and how it has affected me. I realise I lost all my lucidity for a few minutes, as though I was not in control of myself, unable to function as a person for a while. It scares me... In fact it scares the shit out of me!

The barman asks, 'Are you all right, mate? You looked a little spaced out there.'

Worrying that he might think I'm on drugs or something, I reply: 'Yes, mate, thanks. I've not been feeling too well to be honest.' I indicate my battered face, 'Took a bit of a whack the other day and haven't been feeling right since.'

'Oh, right,' he says. 'I see.' But I'm not too sure if he actually believes me as his suspicious expression hasn't changed.

I think it best to drink the water quickly and leave the premises. I can't stand people staring at me and thinking I'm no good when they don't even know me or my situation. It's just another thing to add to the list of things that get on my bloody nerves.

The fresh air now feels good on my face and I walk the streets aimlessly. I spy a cash machine and remembering that I need to replenish my wallet, I draw out the maximum my card will allow, two hundred and fifty pounds.

I am about to put the cash into the wallet but hesitate for a moment. I look at the quality of the leather which was a birthday gift from Jenny recently. It has my initials embossed in gold italics at the bottom right hand corner. I empty it quickly, taking out all the credit and debit cards, discount cards, the odd receipt and all the other bits of shite that somehow have ended up in there. Stuffing them all loosely into my pocket, along with the money, I throw the wallet into a waste bin which I find a couple of metres along the road.

I walk quickly away, and taking my phone from my pocket and using the Google Maps app, I am able to finally find where I am. I see that I am not too far from the British Museum and so head in that direction, using the map on my phone as I walk. Eventually I get to the building where I can see masses of tourists making their way up the steps and stopping to take photographs and buy hotdogs from a stall that has been set up near to the street.

The sense of claustrophobia hits me once more and I know that if I go into the building I will have another panic attack, just like the one I had when I left Agnes Carter's office. I can't let that happen again, but even the thought of it nearly sets me off once more and I stop and take a few deep breaths before I continue on my journey, wherever it is taking me.

I know that the hotel is just around the corner but the last thing I want to do right now is go back and sit in my room all day. I need to do something practical. I need to get my life organised, but it is so hard when there are people staring at me all the time. I can see them as they pass me, looking at me as though I'm some kind of weirdo or something, constantly staring at me and saying things about me as they pass. I know that I look a mess, courtesy of Jerry's punch to my face a couple of days ago, and I know that it's probably hard for them not to stare at me, but why are they all talking about me and laughing at me too?

Do they think it's funny that my face looks like this? Do they find it hilarious that my life has gone to rat shit in the space a few short days? Losing my wife, my job, my dignity and even, to a certain degree, my self-respect. Well do they? Do they? Answer me that.

Agnes Carter comes into my head again. I think about what she said when I left her office, what was it, less than an hour ago? Will she really read my work? Did she mean it? Was she just pacifying me to get me out of her office and away from her? It was pretty clear that she must have said something to the receptionists about me because of the way they were looking at me when I left the building. There's no doubt about it.

Yes, the more I think about it the more I know that she's been having me on. She has no intention of looking at my work, none at all. How can people do things like this? Say one thing but mean another. Well, it's her own fault if she misses out because I'm sure that someone else will take it on and then she will be crying because she's missed out on the opportunity to represent me. It's her funeral, I suppose. But then she was the one I really wanted. I've seen what she can do for other writers and I know that if she just gives me a chance then she will see that she's on to a good thing.

I turn around and start walking back towards Soho. I need to speak to her again. I need to tell her that I won't be fobbed off. I'm no fool. I'm certainly not that. So she shouldn't take me for one.

The walk back takes me twenty minutes and once again I find myself standing at the front of the building that houses Carter, Mayhew and Bell. I now know they are on the sixth floor and that I needn't linger in the reception foyer on the bottom floor like I was forced to do earlier. I do not have to go through those two idiots looking at me suspiciously again and having to engage in conversation with them.

But something stops me from going in straight away. For a minute or so I stand there, looking at the front doors, trying to summon up the courage to enter. I'm scared that the sense of claustrophobia will come back. I am scared of another panic attack happening and making me shake and say the wrong things. In fact, I'm scared of everything.

I must overcome this irrational feeling of dread. At least I have the sense to realise it's irrational and this understanding gives me the mental strength to go in. I open the double doors and stride confidently to the left of the reception desk and to the bank of three lifts, one of which has it's doors open.

It takes a second or two for the security guard to realise that it's me and that I have returned, but his reaction confirms my suspicions that he has been given instructions not to let me into the building, should I return.

He starts to move toward me.

'Hey, you!' he shouts. 'You! Stop! You can't go up there.'

I step into the lift and he enters behind me. I press the button for the third floor and then the sixth. I see the receptionist pick up her phone as the doors close behind us.

I am now alone in the lift with the security guard and all of a sudden, his demeanour turns from one of controlled aggression to one of nervous timidity. I don't know what type of figure I am cutting at the minute but there must be something in the way I look that disturbs him greatly (he would later say I had "the eyes of a madman" and, to be honest, he may have not been too far from the truth).

'Now come on, sir,' he stammers, 'There's no need for any funny business now, is there? You need to leave the premises immediately. My colleague will be calling the police.'

'Police?' I ask him, shocked. 'Why on earth would she be doing something like that?'

'We have instructions not to let you into the building,' he replies.

I can't believe what I'm hearing and am about to speak when the doors open onto the third floor. I can see office workers going about their business, none of them caring or looking over in our general direction, which suits me fine. I take hold of the guard and with all the strength I have, I throw him physically from the lift.

He is taken completely by surprise and stumbles and falls onto the carpeted floor in front of me. Now some of the people look over and I can see that they are shocked at what they see. A middle aged security guard on his hands and knees on the floor and what looks like a right headcase staring at him menacingly from the sanctuary of the lift.

The doors close as I see one or two of them move over to help him and the lift continues up to the sixth floor.

I feel that I'm smiling. That taught him, the interfering little bastard. This has nothing to do with him.

And then I wonder why they would call the police. Surely not. Maybe they should now, though, seeing that I have technically assaulted a security guard. But why call them before I have done anything wrong?

With this question still pondering in my head I step out of the lift and head towards Agnes Carter's office. I pass the good-looking, busty, sixth floor receptionist and try to catch her eye, but I can see from the expression on her face that she has no intention of smiling at me this time.

She rises from her chair and is about to call to me to stop when I see the door to Agnes Carter's office open and she comes out, a rather strange looking old man accompanying her.

'Miss Carter,' I shout. 'Miss Carter.'

She turns and sees me, a look of what I can only describe as total horror upon her face. I can tell that she never expected me to come back, well not so soon anyway.

She stops. I can tell she doesn't know what to say and for a moment, neither do I. It seemed a good idea to come back. A good idea to make sure that she wasn't making a fool out of me and to re-emphasise the quality of my work, to tell her that she should read it straight away, but now that I am here, standing in front of her and the man who I assume is Peter Coconut, or whatever the bloody hell she said his name was, I feel that I may have made a big mistake.

'Yes?' she says. '...Mister Summers. What do you want?'

Stuck for what to say I mumble, 'I was just making sure that you were okay with what we spoke about before.'

Even to me it makes no sense, so I've no idea what she must be thinking.

I can see from her expression that she is not too happy at me being there and interrupting what she considers is an important meeting with a well-respected client.

'Mister Summers,' she says. 'I told you before that I would take a look at your work but you were only here an hour or so ago. You can't pester me like this.'

'Is everything all right?' asks the coconut guy, looking from me to her and back again.

'I'm sure it is,' replies Agnes Carter, not taking her eyes from me. 'Mister Summers will be leaving now, won't you, Mister Summers?'

I sense someone behind me and I turn around. It's the security guard. I can see that there is a hole in the knee of his right trouser leg, probably from the friction as he flew along the carpet. I can just make out red skin on his kneecap through the hole. His face is sweaty and flustered and he is by no means too happy.

'You must come with me now,' he says, putting his hand on my shoulder like Dixon of Dock Green or someone. I'm close to saying 'It's a fair cop' to complete the scene. But I don't.

I can't really remember too well what happened next, but I do recall a lot of screaming and shouting. I think it came from the reception girl with the nice cleavage if I remember correctly, but then it could have come from Agnes Carter. All I do know is that I don't like people touching me when uninvited. I remember the walls closing in on me and the sense of panic returning. I remember people shouting to call the police, but I have no idea what for. I remember rushing as fast as I could to the stairs at the side of the lifts and virtually bouncing down them to the bottom floor. I remember having to get out before I died of suffocation and I remember running through the reception area, out into the street, and hurling up bile and water, which burned my throat as it violently left my body, into the same wheelie bin I had deposited my breakfast into only a short while earlier…

I find myself running through the streets as fast as I can, with no direction, not knowing where I am running to. I pass people and they look at me and talk about me, whispering words I can't make out but I can hear their voices long after I have passed them, each voice adding to the next until all I have is a cacophony of noise inside my head. I run into a park, I can't tell you which one it is, and I run until I can run no more.

I find a bench and sit on it and the next thing I know I am being woken by a little old woman who tells me that I have been sleeping and have been babbling and shouting out as I slept.

I have no idea what is happening to me. It scares the living shit out of me and I think that what I really need right now is a doctor, but I still have a sense that there are things I need to do before I go and find one. I feel empty and alone. A man with no friends. A man with no purpose in life, now that my plans are all gone. All of them. Wife, job, the lot. And there is no way that Agnes Carter is going to give my novel the time of day now, and who can blame her?

And Jesus! How my head hurts.

The sleep has helped to clear my head slightly and being in the park, away from confined spaces makes me feel a little more relaxed and less nauseous. I stand up. I need to get myself a drink and something to eat because I feel very hungry all of a sudden.

I thank the old lady for her concern and walk away towards where I can see a roadway. I need to get my bearings and make a decision on what I am to do next.

There is no doubt in my mind that the offices of Carter, Mayhew and Bell would have contacted the police about what I did in there a couple of hours ago. The sad thing is that there is no escaping any of it really. They have my name (although she may pass it to them as Alec Summers, the stupid bitch) and they probably have CCTV footage of me entering and leaving the building along with a statement from the security guard, who I kind of assaulted, complete with the evidence of torn trousers and grazed knee. And, let's face it, it'll be hard to deny because just how many head-case northerners with two black eyes are roaming the London streets right now?

I'm on a loser here, no doubt about it!

As I approach the roadway the usual hustle and bustle of the crowded streets gets closer but this time my thoughts are clear and not thrown into disarray like earlier. Two panic attacks in the space of a few hours. I've never had them before. Never. I've always been a laid back kind of bloke until very, very recently. I find it extremely odd that my persona has changed so much. I seem to have lost the ability to keep my mouth shut and the things I've always wanted to say and the things I've always wanted to do have now manifested into reality and I can't seem to help myself. In fact I've taken great enjoyment out of it to a degree, if I'm honest.

There was nothing more satisfying than shitting in McGuigan's desk drawer and nothing gave me more of a sense of revenge than pissing in John Michaelson's car. Telling Henderson and the others what I actually thought of them was also spiritually uplifting and even, if I think about it, a big release of pent up frustration that felt really, really good. All these things that I would have thought about doing and even maybe joked about doing to my friends and colleagues but I would never have actually done them. But I have.

And it's turned my life to shit.

I know now why people say things but don't do them. Consequences. Pure and simple. It's good to let off steam, no doubt about it, but to actually do the things we say we want to do only leads down one path and that is the path on which I now find myself. A one way street to self-destruction.

The noise of the street washes over me and I start to feel human again. It looks like the little nap I've taken on the park bench has recharged my batteries, so to speak, and I now feel relatively normal. I check the map on my phone and find that I am around the corner from a tube station. I contemplate using the underground to get to Euston Station and going home but write off using the tube. If I have another panic attack down there it could be fatal. And then I remember I have my hotel key in my pocket and need to check out if I'm going to do that. I also need to collect my laptop from the room but I'm a little worried that the confined space of the hotel room may set me off with another bout of claustrophobia and have another panic attack.

I see a taxi and stick out my hand. He pulls over.

'The Royal National Hotel, please,' I say as I get in.

The taxi driver looks at me suspiciously through the mirror and hesitates. 'Don't worry,' I say taking out my money and showing him the wad of banknotes, 'I can pay you. I might look like a tramp but I'm not one.'

This seems to pacify him but he says nothing and pulls out into the traffic.

As we drive along, I wind the window down and let the breeze blow into my face, closing my eyes in the process and attempting to make my mind go blank, which remarkably I am able to do, and before I know it, we are pulling up outside the hotel. I give him a twenty pound note, tell him to keep the change, and get out of the taxi. I have no idea how much the journey has cost but want to get out of the vehicle as quickly as possible and into the openness of the street.

Walking past a coach full of arriving tourists, I move quickly to the reception area and am happy to see that there is no-one waiting to be served. The same young

Eastern European girl is there and she smiles at me as I approach, although her eyes take on the wary look that I have grown familiar to over the last day or so when people look at me.

'Can I help you, sir?' she asks politely.

'Yes,' I reply and try my best to put on a smile that could hopefully be described as charming. 'I need to check out early. I don't want any kind of refund or anything, that's okay, but I just need to leave, something's come up you see and I need to get home.'

I'm aware that I'm babbling and I can see that she is having to concentrate to make out what it is that I'm saying. I'm maybe talking a little too quickly and in an accent that is hard for her to understand. I slow down and continue, taking out the room key and placing it on the counter.

'You see, what it is,' I say. 'I have left my laptop in my room and I need to collect it....'

'Well why don't you go and get it and then you can check out?' she says. I know she is trying to be helpful but does she really think that I'm so thick that I hadn't thought of doing that?

'I can't,' I say. 'I've been having panic attacks and I'm worried that I'll have another if I go back to the room. I'll give you twenty quid if you get someone to collect it for me.'

She can see the panic in my eyes but I don't think she fully understands what I'm getting at. She tilts her head slightly to confirm that she doesn't have a bloody clue what I'm going on about.

'Is there anyone else I can speak to? Someone who understands English?' I realise straight away that this sounds rude, but after the day I've had, I really couldn't care less.

She looks at me, affronted.

'I can assure you that I speak very good English... sir.'

Oops. Someone else I've upset. The list is growing by the minute.

'Oh, bollocks,' I say. 'Just take the key will you.'

I push the key toward her and turn around. I will sort out the laptop when I get home. I'll ring them. They can send it on or something. I can't be bothered with this right now.

I leave the building and head for the train station.

London may be the centre of the universe for some people but for me it has just been a total nightmare. I thought it was a good idea to get away for a while, to go somewhere where I could sort out my head and get things straight, to plan my next steps, so to speak, but it has turned into the trip from hell. I wouldn't be surprised if the police are even looking for me right now after what happened at the agent's offices. An APB, or whatever they call it. Or is that just in America? I'm not sure.

As I walk along the street, I get the feeling again of people staring at me. I'm aware that I may be being paranoid but it still doesn't stop the feeling. I can sense the world closing in on me once more and it is a constant effort to stop another panic attack from happening. It's becoming a struggle which I'm continually fighting against. It's stopping my ability to think rationally and although I know this, I can do nothing to prevent it from happening.

I get to Euston Station and go inside the concourse. Ignoring all those around me I look at the massive electronic board and see that the next train home is an hour and a half away. It will have to do. I will just have to wait.

I head to the ticket office and purchase a single ticket at an astronomical price.

'Why don't you get a return ticket?' asks the British Rail ticket seller, or whatever they are called now. The rail industry confuses me a little these days. 'It's only a couple of pound more.'

'Why's that?' I ask. 'Its costing me nearly fifty quid to go one way but then only another two quid to do the same journey in reverse. It makes no sense.'

'It's a super saver return. Works out cost effective in the long run.'

'I don't care if it's a super duper whooper saver return,' I reply sarcastically. 'It's still bloody ridiculous. And anyway, I have no intention of ever coming back, so it's just the single if you don't mind.'

He looks at me with that same look as all the others.

Contempt.

'All right, mate,' he replies, 'I was only trying to help.'

I take the ticket and walk away. I'm not too sure but I could swear that he whispered 'Wanker' under his breath as I turned around but I can't be certain.

I look at the masses of people in the concourse. It is exactly like yesterday, some sitting around, others standing staring at the board, waiting for their platforms to be announced so they can rush and push each other in a wild attempt to get to their allocated seat before anyone else, as though the train will set off before they get to it, leaving them stranded in this hellhole. It always makes me laugh, just like at airports when everyone gets up and pushes to the front to board the plane, when they all have reserved seats. Totally makes no sense to me at all.

I stand for a minute or so observing them, and am happy to realise that I have now calmed down. I no longer have the feeling of claustrophobia and paranoia. Maybe it's just London that has made me feel that way, something about being in this massive city that triggered it all off. However, I can't be sure and I'm worried that these feelings could return at any point, stronger and without warning and so I decide to leave the station and find somewhere else to wait.

I turn to the left and head towards the steps that lead down to the street to the right of the station. As I do so I pass the homeless guy who has now returned to his favoured spot and recovered the plastic cup that I kicked down the steps only a day ago. He is sitting with his head bowed and as I pass he looks up slowly and for a second our eyes meet. There is a momentary look of recognition on his face but I can tell that he is spaced out and although he feels he knows me from somewhere, thankfully he can't remember where or why. He gives up trying to remember and bows his head once more.

I carry on down the steps and see a pub across the road. The Royal George. There are a few empty seats on the benches and table outside and I decide I might as well have a pint while I wait for my train.

I go into the pub, which is quite full, and walk up to the bar. A barmaid wearing all black with long, straight, jet black hair, black eyeshadow and black nail polish, with piercings in her eyebrow, nose and cheek (believe it or not) steps forward to serve me. She reminds me a bit of Morticia Addams, only less pretty.

'What can I get you?' she asks, with a smile that looks out of place on a face that is designed to be miserable.

'What do you recommend?' I ask, looking at a row of cask bitters that they have for sale.

'Oh, I don't know,' she replies, uninterestedly. I can tell that she really couldn't give a shit what I want. She just wants me to make my mind up.

There is Spitfire, London Porter, Chiswick, Bombardier, London Pride and a couple of others that sound just as pretentious and naff.

'Which is your most popular?' I ask.

'London Pride,' she answers and I nod for her to pull me a pint.

'That's four pound sixty,' she says as she places the rather flat looking ale on the bar in front of me.

'Four pound sixty?' I say. 'I only asked for one.'

'That is for one,' she replies seriously and I hand over a fiver.

'You might as well keep the change,' I say and turn to find a table.

No sense of humour some people!

Outside I find an empty table at the end of the row and sit down, facing the roadway. I watch as people pass, going into and out of the station and finally I find that I am able to relax. I take a sip of the beer and wince at the taste, or lack of any taste, more like. It really is piss poor. London Pride? Believe me, London has nothing to be proud about regarding this particular beverage, but I drink it nevertheless. After all, it's cost me a fiver!

The traffic down this road is quite calm, but I can see the traffic lights to my left where it looks a lot busier and I'm happy that it is not too loud here, where I'm sitting. A group of people on the table to my left laugh loudly at something one of them has said and I turn to look at them. A young man of around eighteen or nineteen catches my eye and for a brief second I think they are laughing at me, but I quickly check myself. Of course they're not. Why would they?

They aren't are they?

I see another young man walking in the side street to the right of where I'm sitting. He is dressed scruffily and has holes in his shoes which are patent leather. His hair, which is straight and looks as though it's been cut around a bowl, is extremely greasy and the fringe sticks to his forehead because of it. In his hand he is holding a plastic carrier bag and is collecting litter from the gutters and placing it in the bag. Strangely, he sniffs each item, each empty crisp packet, discarded receipt and empty polystyrene food container before he puts them, very delicately, into the bag. He is getting closer to where I'm sitting and I avert my eyes away from him. I hope he walks by because I can't be arsed with conversing with another bloody nutter today.

He gets ever closer and now he is only a few feet away from me. He looks over and approaches me, standing on the other side of the short metal fence that separates the pub premises from the street itself.

'Hello,' he says in a voice that is a cross between Mr Bean and John Major. His lips are extremely thick and there is something very strange about his teeth. Despite his quite disgusting appearance, his teeth are the whitest and most perfect I have ever seen and I find myself staring at them.

'Hello,' I say back hoping that he will quickly piss off and leave me alone.

'Do you have the time?' he asks.

I look at my watch.

'Nearly five o'clock,' I reply.

"Thank you,' he replies and walks on, back into the gutter to carry on with his one man crusade to clear London's streets of rubbish.

I sip my quite terrible beer and sit back. I laugh to myself. This place. My God.

I can feel the occupants at the table to my side looking at me again. They have seen this exchange and they are all staring at me, as though this headcase is some kind of mate of mine. Why are they staring at me? What is the matter with these people? I can feel everything closing in on me again. My head is starting to pound and I am finding it hard to catch my breath. Everyone passing the front of the pub is looking at me and whispering about me as they go by.

I can stand it no longer and stand up. I run down the street, away from the pub, away from these people and away from the station. I cross the road near the traffic lights and can hear cars screeching to a halt as they try to avoid hitting me. I hear people shouting abuse at me as I run.

I run and run, heading I know not where. Heading anywhere.

Anywhere but here. But here is always where I end up.

I run and run until my lungs feel like they're going to burst and my legs feel like lead.

Chapter A9
Mosquitoes

It is Tuesday so therefore it must be another group therapy session. I know that both Mister Andrews and Doctor Spectacles think they are doing me good but I'm not so sure. I suppose there may be something in it as a few short weeks ago they had me pretty much handcuffed all the time because of my unpredictability and my apparent violent tendencies. That doesn't happen anymore and I'm able to control my feelings a little better. Maybe it's down to these sessions, but I'm more inclined to think that it's simply the medication, my little chat with Scabby Eddie or that I've simply surrendered.

They think all this is in my head. They think that I can control my emotions if I really try hard enough. They say that I need to be able to go back to the way things were a couple of years ago when I used to let things wash over me, but it's a constant struggle. For some reason I've lost all my social skills and struggle to hold my tongue. It has lost me all my friends and made me exactly one of those people I have treated with contempt. By being irritated by people, I have become the source of other people's irritation. Ironic really, when you think about it.

I look around the room and see that Scabby Eddie is scratching away at his shin again, his trouser leg rolled up to his knee. Flakes of his skin slowly drift to the floor leaving a pile of white human detritus there, in contrast to the dark brown carpet. Whereas a couple of weeks ago I may have shouted over that he was a dirty bastard, now I hold my tongue.

It doesn't stop me thinking it though.

His master and commander, the dwarfish looking Charlie Jones sits there quietly and occasionally looks over at me with a scowl on his face. I so want to go over and punch him or ask him who the fuck he thinks he's staring at, but again I resist. I merely turn my head away from him, ignoring his looks. Sitting next to him is Vivien, his tattoos seemingly shining brightly today which is extremely creepy. I look up to the ceiling and notice that he is directly under one of the spotlights and so accept this as the reason for this and that he is not, in fact, some kind of demon, despite looking like one.

A new guy has joined us. He has just been admitted and I have immediately christened him "Dandruff Duncan". He looks around thirty years old and has straight, thick looking brown hair. Every time he turns his head, flakes of dandruff rain down onto the shoulders of his dark brown jacket, like some kind of Scandinavian snowstorm or one of those Christmas ornaments you shake and it looks like its snowing on Santa or something else Christmassy. A snow globe. That's it. Snow globe. I wonder if the guy has ever heard of Head and Shoulders shampoo. I make a mental note to mention it to him later if I get the chance.

Doctor Green (aka Doctor Spectacles - I have now stopped thinking of him as such in an attempt to behave myself) looks around the room at the bunch of us and his eyes finally stop on me.

'Alex,' he says with a smile. 'How has your week been?'

I sincerely hope that I can behave myself today. I really do. But sometimes it's so hard and sometimes it's just too tempting to say what I'm thinking. I hope I'll be able to hold my tongue.

'Fine,' I reply. 'Nothing eventful has happened to me since the last session. All quite boring really. You might be better off talking to one of the others.'

I am aware of nurse Brian or Ryan (I still haven't found out what his real name is) standing at the doorway looking over at me, like some kind of prison guard. I can tell he still feels that I'm the one he needs to keep a close eye on out of the group, that I'm the one prone to blow up at any time and cause trouble. At this moment, trouble is the last thing on my mind. I just need peace. I have learned that as long as I accept that there are always going to be idiots and fools in the world and that I can do nothing about it, that that particular fact is just that, a fact, then the sooner I may find the peace I'm looking for. I'm not sure what's caused this sudden change in me. It could be that the medication is finally working or it may be because of these sessions, and the time I've spent in Mister Andrews' office. I'm prone to think that it's more than likely to be my little chat with Scabby Eddie the other night. Whatever it is, my outlook on life seems to be changing. I no longer feel that I need to be running.

'Oh come on, Alex,' says Doctor Green, looking over those spectacles at me. 'I'm sure that you can contribute more than that. Maybe tell us how you are feeling right now.'

I look at him and sigh. I can see that all eyes are on me, and the group are waiting expectantly for some words of wisdom. Or maybe they are hoping that I might kick off again, like I have often done in the past, and give a little excitement to the proceedings.

I decide that I'm going to say it how it is. I'm going to let these people know what's been going on in my head for the past few months.

'Can I tell you a bit of a story?' I ask.

Doctor Green leans forward expectantly.

'Yes,' he says. 'By all means.'

The room is suddenly quiet and they all stare at me. Even Ryan/Brian looks interested. I feel like a singer or a comedian on a stage about to start a performance. I feel good. I find I like the attention.

I clear my throat loudly and, like Doctor Green, I too lean forward in my chair.

'I went on a camping trip once... years ago,' I begin, 'when I was very young. I was in the scouts... or it may have been when I was in the cubs, I'm not too sure. We went to some camp site in the south of France, I can't remember where exactly but I remember I had to share a two man tent with this other kid, Nigel. I didn't mind so much because he was a nice lad. A bit quiet for me, but nice, you know. I remember it being really hot and that it was very uncomfortable trying to get to sleep at night so we left the tent flap open to let in some cool air. Well, when we woke up after the first night there, Nigel looked like he'd contracted the plague or something. His face had loads and loads of mosquito bites. All over it. He was absolutely covered! He looked hideous. We counted seventy four bites in all. Seventy four! Can you believe that? The funny thing is that they had left me alone. I was completely bite free whereas Nigel, the poor sod, was bitten to buggery. His face was a total mess. I could never understand why they had left me alone and had all gone for him. It didn't make any kind of sense to me... it still doesn't... why that would happen, because I hadn't used insect repellent neither.

'Well, what's happened to me lately... well I feel like it's as though those bloody mosquitoes have come back to make up for not getting me all those years ago. To have a go at me, as though they've realised their mistake and are now hellbent on getting me. They've been buzzing around in my head and ears.

'You see... I see it's as though all this that's happened to me, all this crap over the last few months, well it's just like those bloody mosquitoes that ate my mate's face. All of them trying to bite me and suck out my blood, suck the life out of me. And I try and try to fight them off, to swat them away, but no matter how much I fight them, they keep coming back. It's incessant. And no amount of repellent will keep them away. It's been a constant struggle for me for months.'

I can't quite believe where this openness has come from and I find it strangely liberating. It's not like me to let all my feelings out, to what is for all intents and purposes, a group of total strangers. I instantly feel calmed, as though this weight I've been carrying for such a long time has suddenly been lifted and taken from me. I look around the room and can see straight away that those with limited intelligence are not impressed with my little tale, but those with an ounce of sense can see what this has done for me.

One of them is Doctor Green.

'Excellent,' he says pensively. 'Excellent, Alex. And how do you feel now? Do you feel that these mosquitoes are starting to leave you alone, or are they still there?'

It's as though there are only the two of us in the room now. I look into his eyes and I can tell he knows I'm being sincere. I'm not just humouring him or taking the piss or something.

'I think they'll always be there, Doc. Sometimes... no not sometimes... every single morning when I wake up, I find myself in floods of tears for no apparent reason I can think of. I know I've been dreaming but you know, when you wake sometimes and you instantly forget what it is you've been dreaming about? Well that's what's been happening to me for ages. Sometimes I'm actually sobbing, as though I'm heartbroken. During the day I occasionally get flashbacks to what I've been dreaming about and it always involves my poor mate Nigel and those bloody insects. Only this time they are attacking me, buzzing around and stabbing at my brain.'

'What do you think it means?' asks Doctor Green, pushing his glasses back up his nose as he sits up straighter in his chair. 'What's your take on it all?'

'Oh, I don't know,' I answer. 'I'm not so sure, to be honest. Maybe things have been getting on top of me. One thing after another. Maybe those bloody mosquitoes are my demons or something. I don't know. You're the doctor. You're the expert. You tell me.'

Doctor Green turns to the rest of the room.

'Has anyone got anything to say about Alex's story there? Anyone have anything to ask him or add to the subject?'

The new guy, Dandruff Duncan, tentatively raises his hand.

'Yes, Duncan?' asks Doctor Green.

'Yeah,' says Duncan turning to me. 'What happened to your friend, Nigel? Did he die?'

Jesus Christ! Another bloody knobhead.

Whereas a day or two previously, I might have had a go at him for asking such a bloody stupid question, which has killed the intense atmosphere dead, this time I find myself smiling at him indulgently. I suppose it's not his fault he's a bit thick is it? He's clearly in here because, like everyone else in this semi-circle, he can't cope with life outside of these walls.

'No, Duncan,' I say. 'The adults put a load of calamine lotion on his face and he was fine. He was left with a few pock marks though, but I don't think he was too bothered about that. They made him look a bit rough and people would leave him alone and stuff after that. He was fine.'

'Right,' says Duncan and I can tell he's disappointed that my friend didn't die. Maybe I should have lied to him and told him that he had.

No that's daft. You have to draw the line somewhere.

I look at Doctor Green and for a second I think he has winked at me. An acknowledgement that I have responded in the correct way. I feel an enormous sense of achievement. That I have faced a hurdle and overcome it. That I no longer need to run.

And what's more, it took no effort.

No effort at all.

Chapter B9
Steve Cram

I run.

Like Steve Cram, I run.

I run like the Devil himself is chasing after me, trying to catch me in his evil grip to drag me further into the hell I am being pulled towards.

And with each step I take, with every pounding of my feet against this un-golden pavement and with each thud of my shoes upon the concrete and tarmac, a sharp pain shoots through my body all the way to my brain until the pain itself becomes rhythmic with the running.

I pass the crowds, barging through them, knocking them out of my way indiscriminately and ignoring the abuse some of them shout after me. I force myself continually forward to God knows where.

I am in constant pain. My head, my lungs, my legs. All vying for the top spot in the pain chart my brain is trying to process.

I have no control over my senses and actions and so I succumb to the pain and fear. I let it control me.

I surrender to it.

But I must get away from the demon on my tail.

I must get away.

CHAPTER A10
A Surprise Visitor

I have a visitor. I'm not expecting anyone because mum and dad are away on holiday and I have no idea who it can be. Nobody else has shown any interest in me since I arrived here.

Ryan or Brian tells me to go to the visiting area and when I ask who it is he replies, 'Some woman, I've never seen her before,' which is a really big help, the knob. (Although I don't say this to him, I'm not stupid!).

I enter the room and see other inmates sitting at tables, talking to their relatives, or whoever the hell they are, until my eyes rest on a familiar face. I instantly want to turn around and walk back out but something stops me. Call it curiosity, call it "for old times' sake", call it anything you want, but something compels me to stay and I slowly walk over to the table and sit down. I cross my arms and lean back in the chair.

'Hello, Alex,' says Jenny.

'What do you want?' I grunt. I am not going to make this easy for her.

'I thought it was about time I came to see you. We need to sort some things out.'

'It may have escaped your attention,' I reply, 'But I'm currently in a nuthouse and I'm in no position, mentally, to sort anything out.'

'Oh, come on, Alex,' she says, 'we both know that you will be out of here soon. According to your mum you're a lot better than you were.'

'So you've seen my mother, have you? She had no business telling you that. It's none of your business how I'm doing.'

'We are still married,' she says quietly. 'Despite all that's happened, I do still care about you, you know.'

'If you cared about me you wouldn't have slept with my friend,' I say. I'm close to getting up and walking out but somehow I want to stay and listen to her excuses.

'Well can you blame me?' she asks, as though all this is my fault. 'You never showed me any attention whatsoever. You were always upstairs in that bloody room, writing that bloody book.'

'It was supposed to make us a fortune,' I say in my defence. 'It was supposed to be for the two of us. So we could both pack in our crap jobs working for crap people and actually spend more time together.'

'Yes,' she says, getting a little worked up. 'I know that. But you stopped living and became obsessed. And let's face it,' she adds. 'It was crap!'

Ouch. That hurt!

All that work, all those hours typing away, editing and re-writing. All that effort. And now she sits here and calls it crap. To my face, sparing no feelings.

I look at her and smile in acknowledgement. For she is right. It was crap. Total and utter bilge that should have been thrown straight into the bin once it was finished. I've looked at it since all this happened and I have to agree with her. I have to agree with Agnes Carter and I also have to agree with young Tania, her assistant who refused to pass it on. They were all right and I was one hundred percent wrong. It was complete shite. Every bloody word of it.

'That's a bit harsh,' is all I can say and even that is said in a half-hearted way.

'Come on, you know it's true,' she says and I just want her to change the subject.

I find my eyes drawn to her nose. What was once so cute and pretty is now slightly bent and a little twisted.

She notices my gaze.

'Are you happy with your handiwork?' she asks.

I do not reply. I don't know what to say.

'Do you remember what you did to me?' she asks, looking hard into my face.

'Yes,' I reply sheepishly, 'I didn't for a while. My mind sort of blanked it out. But it came back to me a few days ago. Maybe it coming back to me means I really am getting better... hopefully. There's a lot of what I did that's a blank to me. But some of it I remember and some of it I knew what I was doing but didn't care about the consequences.'

'So you didn't remember breaking my nose... smashing your knee into my face after you'd attacked John?'

John. Her speaking his name makes me feel physically sick.

'No,' I reply. 'I didn't remember doing that at all until very recently. But it's all come back to me now.' I look at her nose again. 'I'm so sorry about that. You know I'm not normally a violent man.'

'What the hell happened to you, Alex?' she says.

Can I see a trace of sympathy in her eyes? I'm not sure, but there's definitely something there.

'I don't know,' I say. 'I suddenly decided to stop suffering fools. I think the punch that Jerry whats-his-name gave me in the pub triggered it off. The things I did... my God! Let's face it though, some of it is actually quite funny. I'd have loved to have seen McGuigan's face when he found that turd in his drawer.'

'Very costly,' she replies. 'You lost all your severance because of that. All those years. Not to mention it was absolutely disgusting.'

'The dickhead deserved it,' I say in defence., but I know she's right. It was disgusting. 'Anyway, my head wasn't right, was it? I'd just been told that my book was rubbish, I was being made redundant and then found you in bed with a so called mate. It was one hell of a bad day and I couldn't cope with it because my brain had been rattled the night before. That's the only defence I can come up with.'

'Not to mention having a wee in John's car. Do you know how much it cost to get the car valeted?'

'I don't really care, to be honest, and don't ask me to apologise for that,' I reply. 'Because I have no intention of doing.'

'Anyway, that's all by the by now,' says Jenny. 'Things have moved on a bit, for both of us. It looks like you're getting better and hopefully this was some kind of temporary thing.'

'Yes,' I reply. 'Mister Andrews thinks so too. That's my doctor. He thinks the knock on the head had a lot to do with it and now that I've accepted what I did and that most of it was my own fault, then I should be able to move on and leave here shortly. Call it temporary insanity if you like… but I think you could call it more a temporary enlightenment, depending on your point of view.'

'Whichever,' she says. She doesn't look that interested on what tag we are to put on the reasons for my incarceration in this place. 'Anyway, we need to talk logistics. The house and all that.'

I raise my hand.

'Before you start you need to get it into your head that I'm not simply going to hand over everything to you. I understand and accept that we are over. Although I'm not happy about it I will accept it. If you want to press charges re the assault then feel free, I wouldn't blame you if you did. But I'm not simply going to hand over my part of the house to your new lover.'

'It's okay,' she says. 'I've changed my mind on that. That was put to you on the advice of my solicitor… and my family and friends, but I thought that it was like rubbing salt into your wounds.'

'That's definitely what it was.'

'Let me make you an offer for your half. Or let's sell it and split the profit. Whichever suits you.'

I knew that she could never be so cruel. I knew that there had to be other people having a hand in it all. I look at her and smile. This is so sad. I once loved this woman sitting here before me. I loved her with all my heart, totally and unconditionally.

But now? Now I know that we can never return to what we had before, and what's more, now that she is sitting here in front of me I realise that I haven't missed her at all. Not one bit. And knowing that makes me realise that it really is over and I feel quite happy about that.

'Okay,' I say. 'Get the house valued, send me a copy of the valuation and we'll take it from there.'

'John has asked me to tell you something. He says... '

'I have no interest in what that man has to say, Jenny,' I interrupt. 'Please don't take it the wrong way, but I really don't want to hear it.'

'Okay,' she concedes. 'I understand.'

'Good.'

There is nothing more for either of us to say. I ask after her parents, she asks after mine. We talk small talk for a few minutes but we both know the conversation is at an end.

She stands to leave and I stand too, facing her. She holds out her hand and I take it, shaking it as though she is some stranger that I am meeting for the first time. It is very awkward. For us both.

'I really am glad you're getting better, Alex.' She says.

'Me too,' I reply.

'Okay,' she says turning away. 'Goodbye then.'

She leaves the room without looking back and I look after her until she's gone, the door closing shut behind her. I leave via the other door, the one that takes me back to the hospital, passing Brian or Ryan on my way out.

As I pass him I stop. He looks at me expectantly.

'Can you do me a favour?' I ask.

'Go on,' he replies.

'Can you tell me your name? Is it Ryan or Brian?'

'Eh?'

'Ryan or Brian?' I repeat. 'I've known you now for a few months but have never been sure of your name. Which is it?'

'Neither,' he replies. 'My name's Frank.'

'Well where the hell did I get Ryan or Brian from?'

'Search me,' he says, shrugging indifferently. 'I haven't got a bloody clue, Alan.'

I laugh and walk out of the room, leaving Frank looking at me as though I'm a complete and utter lunatic.

Which is probably exactly what I am.

CHAPTER B10
The London Side Streets That You Slip Down

I carry on running as though my very life depends on it. The muscles in my legs ache and my throat and lungs burn like you would not believe.

Eventually I stop because I can run no more. The energy is gone. I am completely sapped... knackered... done in.

I find myself in the familiar territory of Russell Square and can see the Royal National Hotel to my right. I have run past it without noticing. I bend over and try to catch my breath, then I stand upright with my hands behind my head with my elbows spread from my body. I heard somewhere once, that it opens up your lungs and allows you to take in more oxygen. It seems to work and after a minute or so I have my breath back.

I amble lazily back in the direction of Soho, not knowing why. I am directionless. Like a ship with a broken rudder going wherever the tide and fate decide to take me. Again I can sense people looking at me and laughing at me and talking about me as I pass them. I can hear their voices getting ever louder in my brain and I want to shout and scream at them all, to tell them to piss off and leave me alone, but I manage to contain myself and keep on moving, fighting against the urge to strike out at them. My head is pounding now. It's like having a lifetime's worth of migraines all at once and I find that my vision is affected. I cannot see anything in my peripheral vision, nothing at all, it is just a complete blur and I struggle to focus.

Keeping my eyes fixed to the front I keep on walking. I try looking down at the ground to avoid seeing people but this just makes me feel even more dizzy and I quickly lift my head up before I pass out. I would be worried but I don't have the ability to worry. I don't have the ability to think or do anything. In fact I'm surprised that I can still keep moving without falling flat on my face.

After a few minutes, or is it hours, I have absolutely no idea how long, I come to streets that seem vaguely familiar to me. I get an extremely strong sense of deja vu as I find myself looking upon a building across the road that I have now stopped in front of. I know it's somewhere I've been before but I can't recall when. The memory is there but my brain won't let me access it.

I stand there for a few minutes just looking at it. It is a tall building with steps leading to double doors at the front and I can see people in the rooms on all the floors, working and moving about and stuff.

Eventually people start leaving the building, coming down the steps at a pace and hurrying down the road in both directions, looking for a tube station or a bus stop, to catch the public transport that will take them home to their silly little lives. A journey that is probably repeated thousands of times by thousands of people. The rat race we call it and justifiably so.

Suddenly I see a face that I recognise, but again my brain will not tell me from where. I know that I know this woman, and the gentleman who is accompanying her is also oddly familiar. Are these old friends of mine? I have no idea, but I know I know them from somewhere.

They come down the steps laughing together and they do not see me. They turn to the right, my left, and start to walk along the street, chatting happily together. I can't make out what they're saying but something tells me, that just like everybody else, they're talking about me and laughing at my expense.

I start to follow them. I keep a good few paces behind them, mixing in with the crowds so they are completely oblivious that I'm there. I'm wracking my brains to remember how I know these two people but the word "coconut" keeps coming into my head for some very strange reason.

They turn down a side street and their pace seems to quicken. My eyes are still preventing me from seeing anything to the sides and I have to focus on the two of them as they move steadily away from me, my tired legs struggling to stay with their pace. My full concentration is now just on keeping up with them both.

We are now the only people on this quiet little street and they suddenly stop and turn around. I stop too but walk slowly towards them. They are speaking at me but I can't make out what they are saying. All my senses seem to be shutting down, my eyes can't see properly and my ears are as though they are either full of wax or underwater, dulling out all sound to mere whooshing noises.

I'm aware that they are shouting at me and that they are not happy with me one bit. I ignore them and shake my head from side to side in an attempt to clear it, to get my focus back and there is a momentary break in the dreamlike state that my conscious has become.

'Why are you following me?' says the woman. 'You are in enough trouble as it is, Mister Sumner. You need to go away now otherwise I will call the police again and have you arrested. This is harassment.'

'Yes,' says the man at her side. 'You should leave Miss Carter alone. This is no way for a grown man to behave.'

His accent is weird. He sounds like some kind of alien from another planet.

I stand and look at them, trying to wrack my brains as to how I know these people.

Then it hits me.

Miss Carter... That's it, Agnes Carter. And Peter Coconut (or something like that). Agnes Carter the literary agent who has agreed to look at my book. My God! What luck to bump into her like this! What are the odds of that happening?

'Miss Carter,' I say stepping closer to them. 'I'm really pleased to finally meet you.'

She looks at me as though I'm some kind of weirdo-freak and takes a step back. The coconut bloke steps between us and holds out his hands as though I'm a threat or something. Why on earth would they think that?

'Keep away from her,' he says in that odd accent that I can't quite place. 'Don't you think that you have caused enough trouble for one day, young man. You really need to leave right now.'

I can see Agnes Carter taking out a mobile phone from her handbag and putting it to her ear. I hear the word 'police' spoken and I recoil slightly. Why on earth is she doing this? I only want her to take a look at my book.

'Have you had chance to look at my book yet?' I ask in as polite a voice as I can manage.

'Of course not,' she shouts over. 'You are a nutcase. There's no way I'm looking at your bloody book. No way at all.'

I'm flabbergasted at her nastiness.

'You have assaulted poor Clive and you have caused mayhem and embarrassment in my office,' she continues. 'The police are aware of what you have done and they will want to speak to you.'

Clive? Who the bloody hell is Clive?

She gives her attention back to her mobile phone and starts to talk to someone on the other end of the line, ignoring me. She looks rather frightened, if truth be told.

Then things start to come back to me. I can now recall all kinds of things but they come at me all at once and in no particular order. A security guard on his hands and knees, a good looking blonde girl with a nice pair of boobs, an untidy office, a beggar outside a train station picking up coins that have been scattered in front of him, a girl with a pierced lip with a weird expression on her face. Henderson, McGuigan, Foster, Michaelson, all of them. And Jenny. Jenny my wonderful, beautiful, slut of a wife, Jenny. All of them thrown at me in a kaleidoscope of images and information that I am unable to process or put into any kind of order.

They are both now shouting at me and my head is banging. Banging and pounding. Mayhem ensues inside my brain as it fights to make sense of it all. I can't stand this any longer.

It's all too much for me to handle.

I'm aware I'm shouting and screaming at the two of them. I don't know what words I'm using but they are not nice, of that I'm absolutely sure. It's as though I'm a robot, being controlled by someone else remotely. Someone evil and vicious with no compassion or thought for anyone else. The words that spew nastily and viciously from my mouth are not mine, they can't be mine because I'm a nice guy. Everyone says so, just ask them. Okay, maybe not everyone, but you know what I mean.

I barge past the two of them, knocking into them and I see Agnes Carter fall to the ground and hit her head on the pavement. Peter, the coconut man, whoever the fuck this guy is, attempts to stop me but I push him away easily. I don't know where the strength has come from but I'm happy for it. And then I find myself in that familiar situation once again.

Running.

Running as though my life depends on it.

I run and run. Darting through the streets of London as fast as I can, going in no particular direction, with no purpose whatsoever. I can't think of anything else to do. I just keep on running, with my head pounding and the Devil and all Hell's demons following close behind me.

CHAPTER A11
Homeward Bound

Apparently they found me the following morning lying in a skip outside an office that was under renovation. I was resting on top of a load of old broken furniture singing "Smiths" songs to myself. I have no recollection of any of it, even now, weeks later. I have no memory of how I got there or which song I was singing at the time, but I could probably hazard a guess if I was pushed.

Two construction workers found me lying there, babbling away to myself. I was soaking wet, due to a downpour in the middle of the night, and just as life had decided to shit on me, the sky had decided to piss on me too. And it all combined to create a great big storm of it, that's for sure. That's how I looked at it later. There was no other way to analyse it.

I was in such a state that they called an ambulance and I was treated for mild hypothermia in a local hospital before the police were called. They arrested me as I was discharged from hospital and took me to a police station somewhere else in the city, the station's name I can't remember. They read out a number of charges; harassment, assault, disturbing the peace, that kind of thing, all of which washed over my head. It became clear that I wasn't altogether "there", so to speak, and eventually, after various doctors and solicitors were called, as well my mum and dad, I was sectioned and carted off to this place.

The first few days here are still a bit of a blur to me and I doubt that I will ever fully recall them. I don't particularly want to if I'm honest. Why would I want to remember all that shit? I wish I could forget the lot of it, but some of it will stick in my head until the day I die, no doubt. Much of it highly embarrassing, much of it totally weird, but also, some of it quite funny. I can't believe I actually did some of those things!

Mister Andrews and Doctor "Spectacles" Green have put it down to a nervous breakdown brought on by stress at work (stress caused by having to work with a total bunch of idiots in my view), the break-up of my marriage and the added pressure I put on myself relating to the pretty shite novel that I'd written. It looks like the punch I received from fat Jerry red-nose (I can think of no other way to refer to him) was the catalyst that triggered the excessive behaviour. When I caught Jenny with Michaelson, I reacted in a way I would never have done before. I would have probably kicked off, no doubt about it, but I would have simply walked out. I certainly wouldn't have shoved a dirty toilet brush down the bloke's throat or kicked the shit out of Jenny, had I been "of sound mind", as some have put it.

Both doctors think that I may be over it now. They think that it was a temporary madness brought on by all these significant life events happening to me all at once. I hope to God they're right. I really do.

Jenny has moved on now. She has decided she wants to sell the house and I'm glad about that. She has had the house valued and it looks like we'll both make a few bob from the sale, which is the first bit of good news I've had in a long, long time, believe me. Let's face it, every penny helps at the moment, what with me losing all the severance pay I was going to get due to being officially sacked for gross misconduct, for shitting in McGuigan's desk drawer. I wish now that I'd done it in his fucking face! God I hate that smarmy bastard.

Mum has told me that she's heard that Jenny and Michaelson aren't getting along particularly well. They have been seen having a blazing row in the middle of Asda apparently. I can't say I'm particularly happy about that. Or sad, really. I just don't care. Indifferent is what you could call it, and having this feeling about them must mean that

I'm over her. It must do. One thing is definitely for certain and that is that I wouldn't have her back. No way.

I have written letters of apology to all the people I upset whilst in London. I refused to do it for those knobheads at work because I wasn't sorry for a single thing I said or did there. I wrote to all of them, Agnes Carter, Peter Coconut (I just called him Peter in the letter, I'm sure his name isn't really Coconut, but I couldn't remember what it was), the security guard I threw from the lift, the toilet attendant I pissed on and even the homeless guy that I had the altercation with outside Euston Station, but I'm not sure if he would have received it.

Agnes Carter even wrote back. She told me that I had severely frightened her and she thought that I was going to hurt her, which I did technically because I knocked her to the ground when I ran past her. She wasn't hurt too much, just a little shaken. The big thing about her letter was that she told me that she forgave me and hoped that I would get better soon. I still don't think she has read the submission, but after taking another look at it myself, I have come to the conclusion that I'm no writer and it was all just a pipe dream in the end.

Mister Andrews said writing the letters may help me to come to terms with everything that happened and would help with the healing process. I'm not sure if it ultimately will, but it probably helps to build a few bridges in the long run. Who knows? Certainly not me. I'm no bloody expert.

I look around the empty waiting room with all the NHS posters telling me to check my bollocks regularly, get myself a flu jab or advising me on basic personal hygiene. Eddie could do with reading some of this shit! All very useful information, but all very uninteresting to me right now.

A television in the corner of the room has a daytime quiz show running. Quiz shows for thickos, in my opinion. Asking questions such as "Which football player, married to Posh Spice, was bought by Real Madrid for thirty five million euros in 2003?". The question would have been fine without the Posh Spice bit, but just to make it answerable for the deadheads on these shows they had to include that little clue. Total crap.

Mister Andrews told me the other day that I could finally leave this place. He came to me on his rounds in the morning to find me sitting in my room by the window reading a book, and told me that he and Doctor Green had discussed my case and that I would be able to leave at the end of the week. At first I didn't know how to feel. I didn't know whether to be happy or sad and so I just sat there and said, 'Oh, okay,' as though it was the most normal thing for him to have said.

I first thought about all the blokes I've met whilst in here and how I had come to like some of them (yes, like them, you heard me correctly). Frank the nurse, who I thought was called Brian or Ryan, Dandruff Duncan, Scabby Eddie and even his dwarfish mate Charlie who I finally allowed not to get on my nerves. Even scary Vivien with his very strange tattoos. I asked him about them the other day and he told me the meaning of them all. A very deep man in the end and not the crazy psychopath that I originally had him down for.

I've said my goodbyes now and wished them all good luck. Dandruff Duncan asked if those mosquitoes have finally left my head and I told him that, yes, in fact they had, which was not altogether totally true. They are still there but the buzzing has become a lot quieter now. I can control them. The repellent is working.

I look up as the door opens and mum and dad walk in. I stand up and mum comes running straight over and hugs me very tightly, as though she wants to physically damage me. I let her get it out of her system and as we break away, dad holds out his hand and I take it.

'Come on, son,' he says. 'Let's get you home.'

Home.

Home, I think.

I haven't got one anymore.

Then the bloody Smiths come into my head again.

That Morrissey.
He's got a lot to answer for!

        THE END

Acknowledgements

Firstly and primarily I would like to thank my wife Dawn for her love and support. I would also like to thank my sister Barbara and my good friend Deborah Parden-Bell , for offering their usual words of wisdom and encouragement during the writing and editing process.

I would also like to thank the rest of my family, especially my two wonderful, beautiful, daughters, Jessica and Sophie whom I love unconditionally.

The support of my family and friends in my writing endeavours is greatly appreciated and it is for you all that I do it.

The first draft of this novel took me four weeks to complete, when I had some free time between jobs in the summer of 2014. I have been wishing to release it for some time but for one reason or another I have held onto it. This work is a break from my normal genre and style of writing and I hope you have enjoyed reading it as much as I enjoyed writing and editing it.

Cover Art by Kellie Dennis at Book Cover by Design.
www.bookcoverbydesign.co.uk
Author photograph by Danielle McKay

Also available - (historical fiction):

The Journal - available on Kindle and paperback from Amazon.

The Absolution of Otto Finkel (published by Vanguard Press) - available on Kindle and in paperback from many sites including Amazon.

ABOUT THE AUTHOR

After service in the Royal Air Force, John R. McKay worked for seventeen years for Greater Manchester Fire and Rescue Service as a control room watch manager, before leaving to take up other challenges including writing.

He lives in Wigan in the North West of England, with his wife, Dawn, and has two daughters, Jessica and Sophie.

He is a keen football fan, enjoys open water scuba diving and is currently adding the finishing touches to a further novel, which he hopes to release in the near future.

He can be found at www.johnrmckay.com

Follow him on twitter @JohnMcKay68

and on Facebook at
www.facebook.com/JohnRMcKayAuthor